Hoarfrost

to

Roses

D.L. Gardner

Hoarfrost to Roses

Contents

Grai

Grai Madison clicked open his pocket watch—a keepsake his grandfather had entrusted to him—twenty-four carats, with a ruby on the latch and his grandfather's initials etched on the cover. He groaned as the thin metal minute hand clicked another notch. Half-past eleven. Close to midnight! He'd been working way too long, completely oblivious to the world outside. No wonder he had a mild headache, and his eyes burned. He brushed back the curl that hung over his forehead and gathered the papers on his desk, filing them neatly in his leather case, which he snapped shut, satisfied. He had everything he needed for the lawyer in the briefcase except for the Will. The tattered parchment written in his grandfather's hand was too personal to file away. Not only was Grai listed as the heir in the legal documents, but Grandfather had included a personal note which was not for anyone's eyes but his own, at least not until everything was docketed and settled.

Grai, My Dear Grandson.

Of all the relatives in my family, you are the one who has remained the most faithful. I love you like a son. You know how I despise the man your mother married. Were it not for him, she would be my beneficiary. However, because this territory has denied women the right to own land, I am leaving all my assets to you. All of it! Don't let that scallywag of a brute lay one finger on that property. You have the talent and the wherewithal to foster that estate to what it once was.

Let the little tribe of Kallam families remain in the valley. They aren't bothering anyone. Protect them if you must. This Territory was their land before we came here.

Make room for the vagabond, maybe one or two of those freed slaves that need a home. They can help you keep the place integral. Find a pretty miss to marry. One who will be good to you and then you be good to her. Don't emulate the man your mother married. Your sweetheart can sew fancy curtains for the windows and tat lace for the tables. Wish I could live long enough to see your children, my dear boy.

Above all, don't forget about the roses. We worked so hard, you and I, to tend them. Their roots survived the fire. They will bloom again, and you'll have your own park, this haven will be an oasis for your soul, as it was mine.

I left you a gift in the root cellar. No one knows about the gold except for Professor Reinhardt, and he already has his share. He's a good person and may even want to help you rebuild. There's enough gold coin in those bags to erect three times the manor that burnt down. You can do it. You've got the talent.

I love you, Grandson. Take care of your mother when you can. Grandpa Cyrus.

Grai folded the letter carefully and sealed it in the inside pocket of his waistcoat. He took his frock coat from the coat rack and put it on, retrieved his derby, patting his hat firmly on his head, and tucked his case under his arm. Before he snuffed the lantern, he peeked into the adjacent room where the banker's secretary thumbed through papers on her desk by candlelight.

"I'm leaving, Mary," he said.

Mary pulled her spectacles off. An attractive middle-aged woman—her lace collar tight around her neck, her mutton sleeves stylish for women older than her—she hung onto fashions that were quickly becoming obsolete. Grai attributed her modesty to being a widow.

"Did you find all that you were looking for?"

"Finally! It took long enough to locate the deed and the Will, I have everything here!" He held up his briefcase. "I honestly thought he had lost these papers in the fire. That the Will was preserved is awe-inspiring! A chance of Providence, have you!"

"Your grandfather kept a close account of his paperwork. I'm not surprised he had all that information in a strongbox."

"Well, now that I have what I need, probate proceedings will cease, and I can claim my inheritance."

"Nine hundred acres, is it?"

Grai used the snuffer to extinguish the lantern and stepped out of the den into Mary's office, shutting the door behind him. He grabbed a stool and sat across from her, resting the briefcase on his lap. The hours he spent searching through paperwork this last week isolated him from the outside world, bottling up his excitement. He had to share!

"I loved that place, Mary. I spent my childhood there. The land is forested with elk and bear, but there's a fertile valley where grandfather farmed and a creek with the biggest brook trout you'd ever seen. This estate will be the perfect place to settle and raise a family—and to share those memories with my children, or grandchildren. Grandfather's property is everything a man could want."

"I thought it all burnt to the ground during the earthquake?"

"The manor did, and a few of the outbuildings. But I can build it again. Maybe better."

Mary raised her brow and tapped the papers she'd been working on into a neat pile.

"Construction is costly, Grai. You do realize property around here is coveted, especially with the railroad stretching its tracks to Port Summerhill. People do strange things when candy is flashed in front of their eyes. Your land will be a prime target."

"Even more reason to protect it."

"You don't understand. Nine hundred acres is a lot of land, land which might be stolen from you."

"How? What are you saying?"

"I'm saying the land might be better protected if you let probate run its course. The estate by law would go to your stepfather. He has influence, people who can help keep the estate intact."

"Except Grandfather once told me he'd sooner someone push him off a bridge than leave Richard Bonneville a single copper coin."

Mary shook her head and clicked her tongue, laughing gently. "You shouldn't continue your grandfather's vendetta. What good is it to take such a hostile attitude? If I remember correctly, your grandfather's anger did nothing beneficial for him. Look how it alienated him from his daughter?"

Grai closed his mouth. There was no sense arguing with Mary Sellers. She was a pleasant person, but sometimes she pried into his life too much. Richard Bonneville abused Grai's mother, and his grandfather knew how his stepdad treated her. Mary Sellers didn't need to know. Family matters stayed within the household. That Bonneville had fathered an illegitimate child should have been revealed before their wedding for they fought every day thereafter.

"I'm sorry, Miss Sellers. If Bonneville had a legal deed to the property, the fiend would level the land, clear-cut the forest, and sell everything. I would feel as if I had betrayed my grandfather's love and let his hard labor go to waste."

"So, what's left of all that labor and love?" Mary asked.

"A few stone walls, rock, and mortar fragments. And me!" He grinned.

She snickered. "Even sentimental holdings will be pushed aside in the name of progress."

"The gardens alone are priceless. Some roses are shoots from our family's garden in England. Some a hundred years old." Grai's voice tapered. He needed to champion the estate but didn't need to convince the banker's secretary.

There were other features worthy of salvaging; A fountain that had been shipped from England, a well Grai helped his grandfather dig, and stone sculptures too many to describe. These things may not have a monetary value, but they had a spiritual value and were personal to Grai. Bonneville didn't know about the dugout, and Grai wasn't about to tell him.

"I loved my grandfather, Mary. Watching him fade away with consumption hadn't been easy. He was the father I didn't have. He took me under his wing for a reason, to continue his legacy. I wouldn't have pursued structural design without him. No one else thought I had the talent."

"Those are foolish words, Grai. We've all recognized your abilities. Another Renwick Jr, your mother used to boast. She was good to you. She deserves a piece of that property."

"She was good to me until Bonneville moved in. After that, she's been… I don't know, incongruous."

Mary shrugged and shook her head.

"I will build a room for my mother, but she'd have to leave him."

When Miss Sellers didn't respond, Grai set the briefcase upright on her desk and leaned over it, giving her a warm smile.

"You are a kind woman, Mary Sellers, and I appreciate your concern for my mother. I know you two are close. But I intend to honor my grandfather's wishes. If Mother could own land, and if it were just the two of us, things would be different. But they aren't."

Mary sighed heavily and frowned. "Times change. You need to be careful."

"Careful?"

"So much ill fortune befell your grandfather because of that estate. The earthquake, the fire, his consumption. What if the same demons he faced suddenly attached themselves to you?" Her frown reminded him of his mother's, eerie and ominous. He listened too often to his mother's soothsaying.

"The property is not haunted. I promise you." Grai smiled. His mother tried to convince his grandfather he was cursed—a conviction his grandfather passed off as superstition.

"Not haunted. Plagued just like so many other dwellings in this town. Something evil exists here, Grai. The dead come back and when they do, they mean ill well for the living."

"Yes, that's what many people in Port Summerhill say."

"You best heed those warnings, Grai Madison."

"I'll do my best to tread softly on their graves."

"Not their graves, their spirits."

"I'm sure the Good Lord gathered their spirits already, Miss Summers."

"Nothing is for sure, young man." She looked up from her work with a stern expression, and Grai lost his smile out of respect. "Do not scoff them lest you lose *your* spirit!"

"And where would my spirit go if I should lose it?" he asked.

She stared at him; the candlelight casting a wicked shadow across her otherwise gentle face. "You know I'm not the one to answer that question."

"Miss Sellers, I will be as careful as I can."

"You're going to do what you will, and I'm no one to stop you. I'm just offering advice."

Grai tipped his hat and walked out the door.

The downpour had stopped, leaving in its place a coat of ice on the road and walkway. Glad he had sanded his leather soles that morning, he took a confident step into the street and began his walk home. He wouldn't tell Bonneville about finding the Will until he spoke with the lawyer.

Gas lamps reflected light in storefront windows and cast shadows that stretched across the narrow street. A wind had picked up, causing an occasional shutter to slam, a sign to creak, and mist to spray from trees dampened by the rain. The ocean rumbled in the distance; the sound captured by a thick cloud cover. He hurried over the cobblestone until the road turned to dirt and the light of downtown faded in the distance. Passing yard after yard of stately homes, wrought-iron fences, and wild roses, their fragrance long since muted in the fall weather, he turned down a remote forested pathway that led to his mother's house. He had no idea someone had been following him until he heard raspy breathing, as if they were running to catch up.

"Grai!" a voice called.

Grai stopped and turned.

With a sudden crack, his head burst. The world went black, and he collapsed as someone tore his briefcase from his hand. Grai gained consciousness, flattened against the ground with a man straddling him, wringing his neck. He couldn't breathe. He gasped, kicked, fought against the attacker.

"Finish it and let's get out of here," someone ordered.

The dagger flashed in the moonlight and the sharp blade dug into his side.

He retched and doubled over in pain.

The man jumped off of him and yanked the knife out. Grai cried in agony. A warm trickle of wet leaked from his gut, his hands darkened when he held them over the wound. Someone heaved him off the pathway and dragged his body into the brush, rummaged through his coat pockets, ripped his pocket watch out of his vest, and the last Grai heard was the sound of his murderers racing away.

The rain woke him. Or was it him? He saw his body lying in the dirt, blood pooled under him and clotted over a wound on his head, his curls buried in leaves, his clothes muddy, his flesh pale, his neck marred with hand marks. Remorse flooded his spirit. He didn't want to die. He was too young to die.

"Grai," he said and shook the lifeless body on the ground. "Get up. Get up to safety before they come back. Move," he urged, though no sound came from his lips. He slipped inside the body and tried to move him from within, massaged his heart to get a beat. Pulled open his air passage, massaged his lungs, held tight the muscles ripped apart from the knife.

"Don't die, Grai," he whispered.

The body moaned, coming to life.

Grai's spirit pulled and prodded and finally got the body to move, to connect, but not to meld. He couldn't fully become one. Something kept them apart, but this would work for now. They staggered at first; the spirit lifting the body's weight. The body's mind was not functioning, and the spirit—fearful—could not think. They crawled through the brush. The spirit led him away from downtown on the only safe road he was familiar with—the road to his grandfather's estate. They would be unscathed in its hiding places until they could unite again—until this near-death state of existence could be reconciled.

Adele moves in

There must have been a hundred people in the courtroom, and Adele never once turned around to see who they were. All she knew is that the smell and heat of their bodies turned her stomach. This session would change her life forever. Her parents had already been tried. Guilty. Today they would be sentenced.

"This should only take a moment," Aunt Eloise whispered in her ear, squeezing her hand. Adele hadn't taken her gloves off, nor had she unwrapped her scarf from around her neck or removed her frock off her shoulders. She shivered despite the body heat that stifled the room. She wore her mourning dress, a black wool bodice, and a skirt that had been her mother's and swore to herself she would never change out of it.

She knew what was coming. There'd be little chance of mercy. The crime had been horrendous. If only she could have waited in the carriage during this proceeding. The cold air would have been a respite, the torrential rain splattering off the cobblestones would have been a welcome release. However, her Uncle Nicholas Barrington insisted she sit with them.

"All rise," a voice said, and Aunt Eloise helped her stand.

The poor woman. This was her sister and here she was helping me.

The judge took his seat, his ridiculous white wig placed on what was probably a bald head, his double chin and spectacles made Adele's mouth sour and her lips twitch.

They brought her mother and father in from the side door. Mother wore what was once a white bodice and blue skirt, tattered and stained. Father wore stripes. The jailors must have treated him inappropriately, for he had a pale and gaunt look about him. Adele bowed her head, glad for the veil that covered her face. She didn't dare meet their eyes, doing so would be too painful.

"Be seated," the judge ordered and after the shuffling of bodies taking their seats, cleared his throat.

"The court has found you, Madam Catherine Cora Johansson and Mister Johnathan Paul Johansson guilty of first-degree murder. I might mention for the record that Jim Marlin Delaney, an accomplice in this murder, has forthwith been tried and condemned as well, and a death warrant is currently being posted even as we speak. Despite your help with law enforcement, Mr., and Mrs. Johansson, as explained to you by your attorney, the naming of this additional murderer does not exonerate you. I sentence the two of you to hang by the neck until dead this Saturday on October 29th, 1879." He looked up at the courtroom. "It will be a public hanging to give resolution to those who knew Professor Reinhardt. This session has ended."

His gavel hit the desk. The judge rose and Aunt Eloise had to pull Adele up from her seat to get her to stand she trembled so. Adele held the kerchief over her mouth and forced back bile from her fragile insides. She had spent the entire trial with her head down, ashamed, hiding her remorse, and hiding the world from her eyes.

She whimpered, seeing her parents strong-armed by the constables on their way out.

Aunt Eloise had to guide her outside with an arm locked through hers. Adele fought dizziness while they waited for Uncle Nicholas and his coachman, Mr. Fernsworth, to drive the team of mules and the carriage to them. Rain thundered onto the awning of the courthouse entry and dribbled into the stream that had formed along the gutters of the roadway. The world cried with her as she wiped her eyes. A useless gesture, as no sooner did she dry them then they were wet again.

"Hurry," Aunt Eloise said, holding an umbrella over the both of them as they trotted through puddles to the carriage. Uncle Nicholas took her hand as she stepped inside, the hem of her skirt now dripping wet. She scooted over as her aunt followed. The woman threw a stole that had been left on the seat over Adele's shoulders and wrapped her arms around her.

"There, love," she whispered in Adele's ear.

The carriage tilted slightly with the weight of Uncle Nicholas as he pulled himself into the compartment and took a seat across from them. The smell of wet wool sickened her—a putrid aroma that would bleed into her memory from this day forth—the smell of abandonment, of disgrace, humiliation, and of death.

"Well, that's the end of that!" Uncle Nicholas grumbled and glanced at Adele. "You're our charge now, young lady. I expect you to live according to our standards."

"Nick," Eloise scolded. "Give her a moment's peace."

"A moment for what, Eloise? To mourn for your foolish sister and her brigand husband? They're guilty as sin, and we all know it. They're getting what they bargained for."

Adele put the hankie under her veil and pushed back the tears.

"And to mourn for them is treasonous. Would you have joined them in their pitiless escapades, Adele?"

"Nicholas!"

"Quiet, Eloise, do not interrupt me."

Adele's aunt breathed heavily and sat back, clutching her coat tightly, and looked out the window. No one spoke after that. Adele didn't blame her uncle for his reaction. Nicholas Barrington lived the life of an aristocrat, and he now risked his influence, wealth, and reputation by boarding the daughter of two murderers. Port Summerhill was a small community attempting to find its place on the map, and her uncle played a huge role in its success. If he suffered because of his wife's family, who knows the devastation. He had much to lose.

"I'm sorry, Uncle," Adele whispered to the man who gazed at her with his dark eyes. No compassion came from lips that were buried under his salt and pepper mustache. A hard man, her uncle won his status with a powerful hand, determined, forthright. He expected no less from his children and even more from in-laws who would live under his roof.

Staying with the Barringtons couldn't be any worse than what Adele had been through, though. She practically lived by herself as her mother and father were always off on some secret mission. They never told her where, and now that Adele had sat through the entirety of their trial, she wished she didn't know. Imagine murdering a man! A professor at that. And to what gain? Why had they killed him? Adele folded her kerchief, fumbling with the corners, fingers shaking as the carriage rolled along the dirt road overlooking the ocean.

They had already been to her parent's shanty in Port Galleon that morning to retrieve all of Adele's belongings. Packed in a single trunk that now bounced on top of the carriage, they transported them to Port Summerhill where her parents were sentenced. Under other circumstances, staying with Aunt Eloise and Uncle Nicholas would be enjoyable. They resided in a pleasant part of the country, atop the highest hill in the thriving seaside town, where you could see the Puget Sound, an inlet of the Pacific Ocean, and part of the Salish Sea.

As far as her own home? She needn't ask what would become of her father's small cottage. Being a woman, she had no rights to any property. Uncle Nicholas would sell it and the money would go for her sustenance. Neither would she see the friends she grew up with.

The carriage slowed as the mules towed it through the wrought-iron gate of the Barrington estate. Adele drew the curtain back and peeked outside. Pouring rain dampened the red brick of the manor and obscured the arched gables and ornate trimming surrounding the eyebrow and bay windows. Two stately columns bordered the ingress, and the stairs glowed white in the dismal weather. A balcony stretched out over the porch way, and cherry wood double-doors provided the entrance to the home. Extravagant, and yet cold. The house stirred a sick feeling inside of her.

The carriage came to a halt and Mr. Fernsworth opened their door.

He was a dark man, one of Uncle Nicholas' few servants. Her uncle paid his domestics well and gave them a clean bunkhouse to live in. Many of the dark people had fled west after the Civil War, looking for a better life, and found one settling in the Pacific Northwest where they now raised their families. Port Summerhill promised a decent existence for those who made the journey. With the talk of a railway connecting this township to the rest of the world, industrialists had already staked a claim. Men of all races joined them.

Adele would have smiled at the stocky middle-aged black man when he helped her descend the step, but she had no smiles in her. Aunt Eloise hurried her to the porch and opened the doors, shaking a volley of raindrops from the umbrella and stomping her boots in the foyer. Adele took off the stole, hung it on the coat rack, and set her hat above it. Proper etiquette demanded she remove her outside wear while in the house. She would have kept the veil on if she had a choice.

Once inside the house, the aroma of freshly baked bread reminded her she hadn't eaten all day, and the sky had already darkened. Uncle Nicholas brushed by her and Aunt Eloise, headed to the fireplace in the living room while Lila, Adele's cousin, a woman older than her, greeted them.

"Adele, you remember your cousin Lila?"

Adele nodded slightly. "Yes," she mumbled.

She barely knew Lila. Her parents had seldom visited Aunt Eloise and her family. As a child, she wondered why, but now that her parents' lives had been exposed for what they were; she understood. She grew up in Port Galleon, a town south of Port Summerhill where the shellfish industry dominated the trade, and where saloons and bars dominated the nightlife—where young men from the countryside would go to work in the oyster beds, drink their wages, and then find themselves shanghaied on a ship to foreign waters. No one went to Port Galleon if they didn't need to, and very few could pull themselves away from its curses.

"And my children, whom you never met," Lila brushed the hair of a little girl clinging to her dress. "This is Maggie, and Peter is there on the davenport with Benjamin. Maggie's five, Peter is ten. I was with child the last time I saw you. Peter follows my brother around like a shadow, I can barely pull him away."

Peter sat stiff-backed on the couch, his hands folded, lips sealed, sitting next to her cousin, Benjamin.

Adele remembered Benjamin from her childhood now an attractive, sandy-haired fellow with olive skin like his father. Benjamin wore a black silk vest and red ascot, his stark white shirt cuffed at the sleeves. A good-looking man, long-legged, but he lacked the poise of her uncle. That comes with age. Benjamin set his newspaper next to him and stood.

"Cousin Adele! It's been years!"

"Indeed, it has," Adele said, avoiding his stare, and the peculiar twist of his lips which she read as either a smile or a sneer.

"What a misfortune that you finally came to us on such tragic…" he shook his head and snapped his tongue, "…such tragic circumstances."

"Supper's set on the table, mother," Lila announced. "We knew you'd be hungry when you got home, so I had Mei Ling cook an early supper."

Adele followed her aunt and uncle across the polished wood

floor to the dinning nook. Stunned by the visuals of the home, Adele gawked at the portrait of her grandparents on the wall—a couple dressed in black standing against some unknown forest, a wolfhound at their feet—a chandelier lit with candles dripping crystals on gold chains; a collection of delicate porcelain figurines dressed in pastel hues dancing on the mantle, and Uncle Nicholas' sword collection above the hearth. Disoriented, this home was much too luxurious. Adele did not belong here. This mansion was the sort of home where you touched nothing and if you breathed you covered your mouth. The dark mahogany walls eclipsed her as if the chamber were a glorified prison. She shuddered at the thought.

Lila gestured to a man in a stylish suit who bowed slightly in greeting.

"This is my husband, Gareth," Lila said.

"My pleasure," he mumbled without a smile and then glanced away as though he'd already seen enough of her. "Shall we?" He strode haughtily to the table and pulled a chair back for Lila.

Adele knew she lacked some etiquettes the sophisticated side of her family swore to, so she took her time eating and observed their mannerisms. A servant, an Asian woman who stood no taller than the backs of their chairs, served the men first. She smiled at Adele as she scurried around the table pouring water and handing out platters of food. She seemed not able to speak English, for when Adele thanked her, the woman only nodded and rattled something in her native tongue.

"Her name is Mei Ling," Aunt Eloise whispered to her. "A particularly good cook. And she washes the linens as well. She's prepared a room for you, and as soon as we're finished dining, you can change your clothes, and she'll wash them."

Adele cleared her throat. Having someone wash her clothes seemed invasive. She hadn't grown up with servants.

"Don't look so aghast," Benjamin said. "Coming out of the

ghetto is going to be a culture shock for you, but we'll see you through this experience. I'd be more than willing to help you feel at home."

Adele looked at him, stunned by his insolence, yet she had no response for him. She had no words for the rest of the family either. She ate quietly, unsure of what she could say, or who she could address without offending someone. The men at the table, aside from Benjamin who kept smiling at her, concentrated on their dinner. From time to time Uncle Nicholas would shoot her a concerned frown, but Gareth refused to look at her. Peter stared. So obnoxious was the little boy's gaping that Lila had to nudge him to eat. Little Maggie had been the only person Adele could relate to. Maggie and Aunt Eloise.

"I hear there will be people from the railroad attending your gala at the hotel, Nicholas," Gareth said, breaking the stiff silence that seemed to have been focused on her.

"The president of the Northern Pacific Railway will be in attendance. I believe he's bringing his wife and a few of his colleagues. Aside from the festivities, we'll be presenting our proposal. You're welcome to join us."

"I may do that. I commend you for pulling this together. Proud to be part of the family that puts Port Summerhill on the map!" He looked up with a broad smile.

"Nothing is set in stone yet. We've tried this before, but I think we have a better understanding now as to what they're looking for."

"What are they looking for, Papa?" Lila asked as she cut Maggie's meat into bite-size pieces.

"For one, better press. That last critic gave our town a poor review. According to his report, one would wonder why anyone lived here. There was also the concern about the natives, and that our state had not then become a territory under the protection of the United States government. I have addressed all those details."

"And the end of the war, no doubt."

22

Uncle Nicholas nodded as he wiped his hands with his napkin.

These matters seemed too personal for Adele, so she finished her supper and asked to be excused. Once Uncle Nicholas nodded, she set her napkin down and left the others. She heard another chair pushed back but didn't look behind her to see who else had left the table.

She stepped outside on the porch to catch the last rays of daylight. The downpour had ceased, and the cloud cover lifted, leaving the fresh fragrance of rain on the lawn and in the woodlands behind the house.

Mesmerized by the peace, Adele didn't notice that someone had snuck up behind her until he locked an arm onto hers and propelled her off the stairs onto the wet grass.

"What?" she gasped.

"Hush now, princess," Benjamin said. Adele glanced over her shoulder at the child, Peter, standing in the doorway watching them.

"I know this is sudden, but you are the most beautiful young thing I've seen in months," Benjamin whispered, pulling her across the lawn.

"Contain yourself!" Adele freed herself from his grasp by the time they reached the gazebo.

"Oh, I'm contained, lovely. I've been waiting for this moment ever since I heard what happened and that you would be staying with my mother and father."

"What do you mean?"

"Your parents murdering that old man. I know what sort of blood runs in your veins, sweetheart. I know about the women in Port Galleon. I want to make your stay here as comfortable as can be, poor thing, now that they disposed of your parents. If you let me, I can help you feel right at home."

He leaned into her, her dress caught between the railing of the gazebo and his body. What was he doing, his mouth nearly touching hers? She drew back further, freed her hand, and slapped him across the cheek. He pulled away with eyes wide.

"How dare you!" she said.

He laughed. He looked foolish with his cheek flaming red where she had slapped him and that bewildered smile on his face.

"Surely you jest, Adele! Port Galleon has no honor. Admit your poor upbringing and accept me."

"You're my cousin. I will never 'accept you' as anything besides that." She ducked away from him and walked back to the house. She could see Peter still in the doorway, frowning. Benjamin grabbed her arm and pulled her back.

"Don't rile me. I can make your stay here ecstasy, or wretched. Your choice."

"I cannot believe you accosted me within minutes of my arrival. Is that what you do to all the ladies? No wonder you've never married!"

He pinched her when he squeezed her arm and yanked her closer. "Where you come from, there are no ladies. You're an offspring of murderers and thieves. Consider yourself lucky you aren't sleeping in the barn!"

She stumbled backward when he released her and turned to the house, straightening his vest as he walked. He lifted his head and slowed as he neared the stairs, ruffled Peter's hair, and stepped inside. Peter paused a moment to glare at her before he followed his uncle indoors.

The Attic

Soon after dinner, Lila and her family left, taking Benjamin with them. Adele relaxed when he stepped into the carriage. Thanks to the Good Lord, he doesn't live here, and that he boards with his sister and her husband! She would no doubt have other confrontations with him, and for that, she needed to prepare herself. With a bit of luck, he wouldn't pester her again. She would have a hard enough time recovering from the trauma of her parents' trial, and of their deaths.

Adele sat on the couch stroking the family's calico cat, her focus on the fire, attempting to adjust to what had happened, and to this new life. Uncle Nicholas refused to bring them back to Port Summerhill that weekend to watch the hanging, claiming he didn't care to have his family exposed to such shame. For that she was thankful. Despite his rough demeanor, at least he showed some clemency.

Uncle Nicholas had changed into his smoking jacket, a rich red satin with gold threads that glimmered in the firelight. How wealthy he and Aunt Eloise were. Every piece of fabric, she noticed, heralded elegance. A far cry from the meager home and cotton and wool clothes Adele had grown up in. She didn't fit into their gentry. She had no wardrobe that would complement theirs. Her name would be on the tongues of the townspeople as the daughter of outlaws. How would her aunt and uncle cope with that? Maybe they would keep her hidden forever, give her the role of a servant. That wouldn't be so bad. The manor was large and roomy, with plenty of nooks and crannies to hide in when she didn't have a chore to do. Solitude was a lifestyle Adele was accustomed to only here she would be safe from carousing sailors and thieves who frequented the streets like those in Port Galleon. She may even be able to hide from her cousin Benjamin.

Uncle Nicholas retreated into the den with a newspaper in his hand, and soon the fragrance of brandied pipe tobacco permeated the air. Aunt Eloise also had changed into her nightclothes and wore a lovely blue robe. She peeked in at Adele from the hallway.

The cased clock next to the hearth struck a bedtime hour.

"Adele, shall I see you to your room?"

"May I bring your kitten with me?"

"Butterscotch?" She laughed. "She's hardly a kitten. She's nine years old. But yes."

Adele carried Butterscotch up the spiral stairwell. Portraits of ancestors hung in gilded frames on the wall—people she had never seen and had only heard stories of. Great grandparents who had arrived from England, and cousins who had settled in New York before the civil war. On the second floor, they passed a row of rooms with closed doors except for one. Beyond those double doors, the walls adorned with blue and gold print, a crystal chandelier hung low above a grand piano. Adele had never seen a piano before, and so she took her time as she walked by, admiring the instrument.

"Do you play?" she asked her aunt.

"Yes," Aunt Eloise said. "When I have time."

"I would love to learn."

"There are many things I need to teach you. Music is only one."

She opened a hatch to another staircase that led to the uppermost level of the home. Adele followed her up the narrow shaft.

"We rarely use this chamber, but the tower is pleasant and overlooks the garden. You won't hear anyone downstairs and I think you'll enjoy the seclusion. Consider this tower your own private space. The water closet is on the second level. We'll have a servant bring an armoire up here for your clothes tomorrow. There was so much else happening this week we didn't get to rearrange everything we had planned. Perhaps over time, we can get you some other furniture." Aunt Eloise opened the door to a room that overlooked the western boundary of the manor.

The room had been dusted recently, the floor swept, and the smell of walnut oil used to polish the cherry wood walls fragranced the area, but the space lacked the warmth of having been lived in. An iron framed bed rested near a bay window, and the only fixture, a roll-top desk with a lantern stood across from it. That should come in handy if she found the need to write a letter. To whom, Adele couldn't imagine.

"I know it's not extravagant," her aunt said.

There were other guest rooms in the house, this Adele knew— they had passed by them on the way. A room in the tower was more fitting for her because of who she was. Out of sight, out of mind she could see it in the apologetic language of her aunt's eyes.

"Of course. Being tucked away in a tower is perfect for someone whose parents will be hanged," Adele whispered, releasing the cat. Butterscotch found her way to the bed, jumped up, and pawed at the cotton mattress. Finally curling into a ball, the cat rested her head on her paws.

"You know that's not how I feel," Aunt Eloise said, wringing her hands. The poor woman's oppression leaked through her worried gaze.

"It doesn't matter how you feel, though, does it? This is a man's world, and that's how your husband feels. I can adapt, for your sake. I'll have to."

27

Aunt Eloise sighed heavily. She didn't mean to be rude, but how could she hold her feelings in after all that had happened? She would burst soon if left to stew. Her aunt tossed her hands in the air.

"I'm doing my best, Adele."

"I'm sorry, Auntie. I do love you and am grateful for a home. I'm going to try to be obedient and not cause trouble. If I want Uncle Nicholas to respect me, I must work for it."

"He's a hard man to please, but he's also a righteous man once he comes to trust you. I know adjusting to this alternative way of life is hard, but you may come to enjoy your stay here." Aunt Eloise opened her arms to her, and Adele accepted her caress for only a moment, fearful of breaking down in tears. Crying any more than she had would be a sign of weakness, and Adele needed to show strength.

"You've been good to me," Adele said and stepped away. "There's something else." She opened her mouth, wanting dearly to tell her about Benjamin's inappropriate advance, but stopped herself. No. She wouldn't. If her cousin found out, she told his mother, he may retaliate. Benjamin frightened her.

"What?" Aunt Eloise asked.

"I… Butterscotch and I would love to have a pillow."

"I'll have Mei Ling bring one up. Sleep well, tonight. I'll see you in the morning," Aunt Eloise said, and hugged her again.

"Goodnight, Auntie."

Once her aunt closed the door, Adele lay her stole on the back of the chair. Mr. Fernsworth had carried her trunk up earlier and had set it against a wall. When Adele opened the lid and rummaged through her belongings, she found all her clothing damp, having been transported through the storm. She pulled her wardrobe from her suitcase piece by piece and draped each article over the chair, the desk, the curtain rod, the lid to the trunk, wherever she could find support to hang them. The chore wasn't difficult, but putting up wet clothes disheartened her, and tears soon streamed down her cheeks. She had no possessions but what was in this chest, no home to call her own, no parents, no one who understood how she felt, and now all her clothes were near ruined. Is this what has become of her life? Is this what being an orphan felt like?

She wiped her tears with her sleeve.

The last item she came to in the trunk was her nightgown. The driest article she had, she lay the cotton lingerie on her bed and looked at Butterscotch.

"I can certainly use a friend right now. I'm beside myself in despair," she told the cat. In reply, Butterscotch gave her a quiet mew and rolled on her back. Adele fell to her knees scratched her belly. "Silly kitty, you look fierce, but you're all hair."

While Adele scratched between Butterscotch's ears and under her chin, a gentle rapping at the door interrupted her.

"Come in."

Mei Ling carried a pillow and bowed before she handed the downy cushion to Adele.

"Thank you," Adele said.

Mei Ling bowed again.

"No need to bow," Adele waved for her to stop. "Do you speak English?" she asked.

"Little. Just a little." Mei Ling's apron had stains and flour on it, and there was a smudge mark of the powder on her cheek. Her hat curled up at the edges and bulged over her thick black hair.

"The dinner tonight was so good. Thank you."

The woman smiled. "Oh, no need to thank me. Cooking is my duty."

"You went beyond your duty. I should like to know how to cook as you do someday."

Mei Ling laughed. "Oh, no need cook. I will."

"No, I would like to learn."

29

Mei Ling laughed and bowed. "As you wish," she said. "With Master Nicholas' permission, then I teach."

Of course. She must ask her uncle's permission for anything she wanted to do.

"I will speak with him tonight, thank you," Adele said, and Mei Ling pivoted and hurried back down the stairs. Adele read Mei Ling's swift exit as a personal rebuff. She pouted when the door closed. Mei Ling meant no offense. Still, the loneliness that came with being a criminal's daughter stung. Would anyone want to be her friend again? Will the stigma of having convicted felons for parents follow her for the rest of her life?

"I would like very much to learn to cook. Manual labor would be a means of redemption for me," she said to Butterscotch. "I must find some way to prove myself. I can't bear for everyone to think of me as a candle to the devil!"

Adele sighed and looked out the window. The garden area needed tending. The beds looked as helpless as she felt, but winter had already claimed ownership to a good portion of plant life. Though some greenery still fought against decay, most of the foliage had turned brown and with the rain, rotted. The laurel, still green, bordered a patio with stone beds in the center. Beyond that, in the distance where the courtyard ended, dying weeds grew tall, and a curious wrought-iron fence peeked through a wall of ivy. The area on the other side of the fence couldn't be her uncle's property, or there would be stone beds and landscaping similar to the rest of the yard. She could see extraordinarily little in that direction, though, for the last hues of twilight were fading into night.

Adele changed out of her dress and breathed freely once the corset and stockings came off. She exchanged the chemise she wore for the nightgown and paced back and forth, hoping exercise would get her blood pumping and generate body heat. Finally, after watching Butterscotch rest peacefully on her bed, she sat by the window and lifted the cat onto her lap, warmed immediately by the animal's fur.

"Being a cat must be so much easier than being a human being," she whispered. "Such a grand life, making yourself comfortable any time of the day and wherever there is a soft blanket to lie on. You have no worries, do you?"

Adele never had a pet before. There were feral cats in Port Galleon, but they were barn cats and hunted rats and mice and would flee from human beings. No one thought to tame them. Cats roaming about outside kept the varmints and pests that fed off of the shellfish at a minimum. Port Galleon may be a poor village, the homes were not grand estates like they were in Port Summerhill and the residents hadn't fancy silk and satin to wear, nor did they have carriages to ride in. Most of them didn't even own a horse or even a mule. There were donkeys and carts to move their goods with, though their primary means of transportation was by boat. Life was not as degenerate as Benjamin claimed. Many good people lived there. Not everyone committed crimes—as her parents did.

She sighed heavily as the ache inside of her took hold again. She missed her home, as poor and run down as their shanty had been, and she despised what her parents had done. Society—and Uncle Nicholas— would have her deny any love she had for them. According to her uncle, the sooner she rebuffed her father and mother for their crimes, the better off she'd fare.

He didn't understand. As sympathetic as her auntie tried to be, Aunt Eloise didn't understand either. Neither of them had anything to do with her family until now. They could have helped during the thin times after steam-powered vessels replaced sails, and ships stopped docking in Port Galleon, taking away whatever wealth the port had pledged. Supplies became scarce then, and even bartering among the residents suffered. Farmland where she used to live was not as fruitful as the vineyards, orchards, and homesteads in Port Summerhill, and most residents in Port Galleon couldn't afford the technology to compete with their northern rural neighbors. They weren't destitute, but someone like her uncle could have helped pull her family out of poverty. If they had, maybe her parents never would have felt the need to rob the Professor.

Ah, well, Adele knew better than to blame her aunt and uncle. Many affairs kept her uncle distracted from family issues. Maintaining his status and influence, managing a hotel, trading stock, and mingling with bankers gave him plenty to agonize over. Why would he feel a need to rescue his wife's sister and her husband from deprivation?

"It's just that if I ever get in a place where I can assist someone, I will not turn my back on them." She folded her arms, thinking about what she had just told Butterscotch. "I supposed that's unfair. Uncle Nicholas consented to care for me. But how can he expect me to spurn Mother and Father? Am I not allowed to love them for who they were to me?" She stroked Butterscotch's fur, examining the many colors of each hair as they interlaced on top of one another, forming the cat's lovely gold, white and black patches.

"They raised me. They loved me. No matter what they did to anyone else." She held the cat close to her breast, rocking back and forth, fighting the sick feeling inside until nighttime swallowed the earth, and moon rays filtered through the window. She gazed outside at the stars.

Her eyes were teary, and so when she saw a stream of colorful lights in the distance, she thought moisture had caused the distortion. When she blinked, the glow did not disappear, so she set Butterscotch on the bed, rose, and found her hankie. She stood by the window after drying her eyes and, with her arms crossed to keep herself warm, stared at the lights.

Beyond Uncle Nicholas' estate, past the weeds and the iron gate she had noticed earlier, the lights moved about on the neighbor's property. Unlike a lantern, they flickered soft and colorful and did not travel as if a candle were being held by someone walking through the garden. These lights moved in clusters, first one constellation over here and then trickling to another place further away—on again, off again. She must have watched for a good half hour as these little clusters of twinkling color slowly made their way into the woods until they faded completely.

She stood by the window awhile longer, hoping for a clue what this strange phenomena was, but there was no other movement or illumination after that. She yawned, shivered, and decided she had too much trauma that day. The stress made her see things that weren't there, and it was time for her to rest.

She returned to her bed, pulled the covers over her head, and with Butterscotch tucked under her arm she fell asleep to the sound of purring.

Aunt Eloise

Adele woke up to the aroma of bacon cooking. Sunlight shone through the window, but a layer of ice crystals glistened around the panes. Though there had been no snow the night before, frost covered the yard as if an angel had dropped a thin white blanket over the property. The freshness of the morning lifted her spirits, and, for the moment, she forgot the calamity that brought her here. She must have slept late as she could hear someone outside chopping wood, and Uncle Nicholas' carriage waited in the drive. She hurried about the room, assessing her clothes to see if any were dry. Few were, so she put on her drawers, petticoat, and the dress she wore the day before over her chemise, laced up her shoes, and quickly trotted down the stairs just in time to see her uncle kiss Aunt Eloise goodbye and the door close.

"Adele, you're up!" Aunt Eloise gave her a broad smile. She wore her long hair down this morning, perhaps so her dark silky locks would dry. Everything had gotten so wet on the trip here. "I was going to let you sleep in, you had such a rough day yesterday."

"I slept fine, Auntie."

"Were you warm enough?"

"Butterscotch kept me warm," she replied and eyed the cat sitting on a mat by the fire.

"She's going to enjoy having you here. No one gives her much attention anymore aside from Maggie. Sit down and let me brush your hair, you've got terrible knots and tangles." Aunt Eloise took Adele's hand and brought her into the back parlor, sat her in front of a mirror, and removed the pins that had held her hair up the day before. As her aunt fussed over her hair, Adele focused on the paisley wallpaper, the hearth, and the daguerreotypes on the mantel, images of her aunt, Uncle Nicholas, and their family.

"Who is this child in your arms?"

"My first child. That's a memento mori, He died at the age of three."

Adele had heard of death photographs before, but to have the body sitting on her aunt's lap, arranged as if the child were still living, seemed jarring to Adele. Such items wealth could provide for people!

"You have always been affluent, haven't you?" she asked.

"Your uncle has taken good care of me. He works hard, and we are rewarded for his labor."

"To have anything you want, or need must be nice."

Aunt Eloise released the last pin so that Adele's hair tumbled past her shoulders.

"I've been thinking, we must get you a vanity for your room so you can groom yourself. One with a mirror. And I suppose we could bring up a davenport. There's one in the guest room not being used. And a rug."

"You don't need to go out of your way for me, Auntie." Adele winced as Aunt Eloise combed a knot loose.

"You'll be with us an exceedingly long time, Adele. Perhaps until you marry. We must make you as comfortable—and as independent—as we can in this household. In return, you'll have chores, and you can help me with my sewing."

"I don't know how to sew."

"My sister never taught you?"

Adele shook her head. "I don't think she knew how."

"Nonsense, mother taught both of us." Aunt Eloise paused for a moment, as if in thought. "Odd. She used to sew when she was your age. Funny how being with a man can…change a woman. Then again, perhaps when she moved to Port Galleon, she became involved in other affairs."

That sick feeling swelled inside of Adele at the mention of her mother and the other affairs Aunt Eloise referred to.

"She kept busy. She worked, you know. In the oyster beds."

"That's not what I was referring to."

Adele shifted on the chair and pulled away from the brush. "I don't want to talk about what happened."

"We *need* to talk about the murder, Adele." Aunt Eloise stopped a moment to gaze at her reflection. "For your healing, and mine. She was my sister, you know. This tears my heart apart as well. Murder," she shook her head and sighed heavily. "And a hanging."

Adele met her gaze in the mirror. For the first time, she realized how much Aunt Eloise resembled her mother, the dark hair and brilliant blue eyes, the pointed nose and dimpled chin. If Aunt Eloise hadn't been a few years older than her mother, they could have been twins.

"It's hard," Adele simply said.

"Yes, I know it's hard. Did you know the man?"

"The man?"

"The man they murdered?"

"Not personally. I knew of him. Port Galleon is a small town. If your affairs weren't public, then people would allot rumors to you."

"And what sort of rumors did they allot toward this man—this Professor Reinhardt."

"They whispered things about him. I don't know. People tried to rationalize why he lived in Port Galleon. They conjectured what kind of professor he was. All I know is that he lived atop the hill overlooking the oyster beds."

"Was he a good natured sort of man?" her aunt asked. "Or irritable? Loathsome?"

Adele shrugged her shoulders and watched in the mirror as her aunt brushed her hair, wondering why she hadn't inherited that reddish highlights both her mother and aunt had. Instead, her curls were dark brown, dull, and lifeless.

"A hermit, mostly, I think. They say he was once wealthy. They say he once was a broker in gold and had a partner, and the two of them made a small mint. Then they separated. No one knows what Professor Reinhardt did with his wealth, he certainly didn't spend any of his money in Port Galleon."

"Perhaps he kept his wealth hidden away. Perhaps that's why your mother and father…"

"They didn't mean to kill him, Auntie. You heard the attorney. They only meant to rob him, I suppose. That's what I want to believe, anyway. That's what I need to believe."

Aunt Eloise closed her lips tight and moved to the other side of Adele. "If you brush your hair more, it will shine. A hundred strokes daily. Brushing will pull the oil in your scalp down into the ends of your hair."

Adele cleared her throat, letting both subjects of conversation drop. She knew about brushing her hair, but she hadn't been taking care of herself lately. She didn't need a lecture, and so she ignored her aunt's preaching. Instead, Adele thought about the lights she had seen the night before.

"Do you believe in ghosts, Auntie?" she asked.

Aunt Eloise gave her a puzzled look. She remained silent for a moment before she answered.

"I guess, in some respects," she finally said. Aunt Eloise parted her hair and their eyes met in their reflection again.

"What do you mean 'in some respects'?"

"Acquaintances of ours have seen apparitions, and who am I to argue their eyewitness accounts?"

"Where" Did they see them all in the same place?" Adele asked, curious whether her aunt would mention the property next door.

"No. I don't know, Adele. I've never seen them. You could ask Mei Ling. She claims to have seen some. There were natives who lived here before us. Settlers cheated them out of their homes and many people believe they cursed this place when they left."

"Do you?"

"I don't believe in curses. I believe each man and woman bring consequences upon themselves."

"Oh," Adele muttered, watching her tangled hair straighten as her aunt brushed it. Her heart quickened at the idea of a curse, as if a curse were the reason for all the ill she's been through lately.

"Who owns the property next to your estate?" Adele asked.

"In which direction?"

"That which can be seen out my window."

"It's abandoned as far as I know. The man who owned the estate was old and feeble. There was a beautiful house there at one time, but unfortunately, the manor burned to the ground, left for the elements and vandals to destroy." Aunt Eloise braided Adele's hair, swirled the braid on top of her head and, using the same pins that were in her hair before, secured it into a bun.

"Where is the man now?" Adele asked, worried about the lights she saw the night before might indeed be a ghost haunting the ruins.

"He died recently."

Adele's eyes popped open.

"I've heard a rumor that one of your uncle's colleagues, Mr. Bonneville, owns the property now. Nicholas has been meeting with the man recently, and I think your uncle will purchase that land soon. Supposedly the acreage will be worth a small fortune when they build the railroad here."

"Does anything unusual ever happen there?" Adele asked.

"Unusual? In what way?"

"I don't know. Just out of the ordinary."

"Not that I know of. There are remnants of the manor that once stood. Ruins now. The rest is mostly forest and a small graveyard. There's a flatland at the bottom of the hill that the men are considering for the train depot, but I have never seen that part of the country. I've never explored the place. It's private property you know."

"How large is it?"

"I'm not sure. A few hundred overgrown acres. It's still wild. Bear, cougar, elk. There! All done." She stepped back, arms folded, and admired her handiwork. "We must introduce you to the gentry's who live around here. You're at that age, Adele. Eighteen, correct?"

"Yes, I'm eighteen. I'm at that age for what?"

"Courting, my dear."

"What man would court me? According to Uncle Nicholas, I'm not worthy of being courted." She regarded the style her aunt created and smiled slightly. She had to admit she looked better with her hair brushed and neatly pinned.

"Oh Adele, that's not at all what your Uncle suggested. He simply doesn't want you brooding indefinitely. The entire family must move past this shame."

"And act as though my parents killed no one and were never sentenced to hang?" Adele looked at her aunt. The woman gave her no response.

"Your cousin Benjamin is coming over this morning to replace some wainscoting in the hall."

"He is? Then there must be something I can do to make myself scarce?" Adele asked, her heart skipped a beat. Benjamin was the last person she wanted to see. "I could gather firewood."

"It's cold outside."

"I don't mind cold."

Aunt Eloise gave her a bewildered look and then sighed. "We can always use firewood. Don't you want to eat first?"

"I do."

The Mysterious Garden

Once she had finished her breakfast, Adele ran up the stairs to her room to change into a skirt that gave her more mobility for gathering wood, one that fell above the ankles. She laced up her boots and put on her wool coat, scarf, and gloves. A carriage stopped in front of the house just as she stepped off the last rung of the stairs, and so, to avoid Benjamin, she hurriedly snuck out the back door through the kitchen onto the storm porch. Mei Ling gave her a confused glance when she passed by but said nothing.

As soon as Adele opened the porch door, a blast of frozen air hit her. Clouds had returned, though they were not low enough to warm the earth. A storm gathered to the north, foretold by gusts of wind that prickled her face. Her nose and cheeks grew numb within seconds. Even the steam from her breath seemed frosty. Icicles had formed on the overhang over the back walkway. Fallen leaves sprouted barbs of crystals pointing in the direction the wind had blown.

Safe from her cousin's eyes, she decided to stay out as long as she could manage the cold. She'd bide her time in the garden and return once the carriage—with him in it—drove away. Hopefully, her aunt wouldn't invite Benjamin for supper.

She pulled her thick wool scarf tighter over her head and covered her chin. The ground under her feet crunched as she walked, but her wool coat kept her warm enough that the beauty and magic of hoarfrost lured her away from the house. Her first thought was to wander toward the neighbor's property and see if she could find where the lights she had seen came from. Exhaustion the night before might have caused her delirium, but she never before had been stricken with hallucinations. She had a young and healthy mind and had stared at the lights for a good long while. She swore they were real.

In her uncle's yard, beyond the stone beds filled with leaves and mulch, past a water fountain and benches covered in frost, a footpath to the neighbor's property ended at a tangled mass of dormant honeysuckle. The vines were thick and in one spot, wrapped around the wrought-iron fence. To open the gate would take a great deal of effort, but she could see a trail surrounded by bramble bushes on the other side. Unable to move any farther than the vines, Adele sighed in frustration and turned around, about to give up. She'd gather firewood from the woodpile near the back door, return to the manor, and face her dreaded cousin. At least the house was warm.

Before she made up her mind, she eyed the same illuminations she'd seen the night before, shining through the foliage on the other side of the fence. Not a white light. The clusters were more of a transparent glow and drifted, floating through the icy bramble first in one spot— then nothing—and then directly opposite from where they'd been.

Determined to find a way onto the neighbor's property, Adele bent back the strongest limb, pushed on the vine with her shoulder while pulling the gate. The rusty hinge squeaked, the branches moaned, and the gate gave way. A whiff of honeysuckle still lingering from summer's perfume caught her as she passed. Her heart raced with excitement.

She let the gate stay open and stepped lightly over the frozen ground for fear of scaring the wonder. If it were a ghost, she wanted to see it. The light rounded a bend ahead of her, and when she came to where it had turned, the thicket ended, and she found herself at the edge of what was once a courtyard. A fountain of magnificent size stood before her. Two tiers of pools in the shape of shells surrounded an alabaster woman holding a water jug. The statue had a cracked hand sealed with moss, now brown and frozen, which also grew the folds of her dress. Ice, frozen twigs, and leaves had blown into the recesses of the pools during the latest storm. Frost coated a row of garden beds to her right. To her left, two privets bordered a staircase that led down a hill to a stand of birch trees some distance away. On the slope, headstones jutted out of the rocky ground.

"The family graveyard," Adele muttered, terrified and yet in awe. She stood quietly, absorbing all that she saw, mesmerized for a moment. What a grand place this must have been in its day—now destroyed and forgotten. She would love to know its history. Who had lived here? Where was this old man's family, and why had they let the property disintegrate so?

Undecided as to what she should explore first, the mysterious light appeared near a garden bed beyond the fountain.

She moved cautiously toward it as the whole of its form came into focus.

What she saw appeared transparent and glowing, shaped like a shadow but light instead of dark. It rolled over what was once a rose bed, and she gasped, for as it moved, the moldy dead roses it hovered over burst with color, brightening everything around it. This was the light she had seen from her window. The flowers budded unexpectedly— red and pink—the most stunning roses she had ever seen, with delicate hoarfrost lacing their petals. Her breath left her as the entire garden lit with color—now yellow roses…and white.

Her gasp drew the attention of the light-shadow figure. It turned to face her. In that transparency, a young man's face stared at her. He had a head of curls, wide eyes and full lips, and an innocence about him. Her eyes locked with his and something inside of her connected to him. A desire to know who and what he was? Sympathy? Intrigue? She wasn't sure what emotion stirred her. Not fear. It was the miracles which he performed that melted her heart and gave her a grave desire to know him.

A sudden gust of wind rustled the trees and blew mist into her eyes, obstructing her vision. When she could focus again, the light-shadow had vanished, and the roses had wilted into muted brown. Only the frost, the cold, and the threat of an impending snowstorm remained.

She shuddered, stunned by what she had observed, and by the drop in temperature. She quickly wrapped her scarf tighter around her head and hurried back through the vine-covered trail to the gate. When she reached the fence she stopped, for there in her uncle's yard wandered Benjamin, calling her name.

The Ruins

Grai stretched out and leaned his head on the masonry wall, whereupon his grandfather's favorite dog had been immortalized as a statue. He shivered as he surveyed what was once a patio, but now only a clearing of broken stone and rubble separated from the courtyard by an arbor of twisted wisteria. The wound in his side pulsated and still bled, though he'd wrapped it with a torn shirt he found in the root cellar. His waistcoat, blood-soaked and stiff, he'd taken off that morning and discarded. With half-closed eyes, he watched his spirit move about the garden, bringing life into the heirloom roses that had once made his grandfather proud—something he had dreamed to accomplish in reality. A useless gesture now in the winter. Pulling his coat tighter over his shoulders, he groaned as a spasm of pain passed through him. If he lived long enough to fulfill his dreams of rebuilding this place, it would surprise him. He assumed his death would come in a matter of days, and then his stepfather would celebrate by selling the estate. The man who, no doubt, paid to have him murdered.

The work of his spirit brought him solace, though, and he enjoyed observing the transformation of dead plants into blooming heirloom roses. He guessed his spirit was performing these minor miracles to please him, to get his mind off death. If nothing else—through his spirit—he could imagine his dreams being fulfilled. For that, he could die in peace.

His spirit slid under the wisteria to the courtyard where the colorful lights of budding roses filtered through the mildewed branches. Grai opened his eyes with a start, surprised that the spirit's work ended abruptly, and the quivering image returned to his side.

"Why did you stop?"

"A trespasser is here in the garden."

Grai moaned. They were after him, still? He tried to move, the pain too unbearable. He swallowed. "How many?" he whispered.

"I saw only one. A woman. A very pretty woman."

"A woman? A spy."

"Perhaps," his spirit answered and looked back the way he had come as if he wanted to return to where he'd been. "She's gone now."

He seemed disappointed.

Grai breathed heavily, his throat still throbbed, and his wound bled. The world would be better off if he just let the executioners finish him.

"I can't hide from them forever. I certainly can't run." He closed his eyes and leaned against the stone again. There'd be no relief for him until he passed, no matter what his spirit tried to do. "We're going to die, the two of us."

"I won't die. Only you." His spirit grinned, making Grai frown all the more.

"That's supposed to be a comfort?" Grai asked.

"In a way, yes. Should you die, we'd become one again."

"I'm not so sure that's true. Look at you. You're a far cry from anything that I am."

"How's that?" his spirit captured Grai's frown and pouted.

"For one thing, you're happy," Grai said.

"I'm free."

"That's what I'm saying. You're free from pain. You don't feel what I do."

"No. At the moment I haven't a body to feel pain, but I do identify with you. When you hurt, my heart hurts."

Grai nodded, a snicker on his face. "Thanks for the sympathy."

He sat up as best he could. His spirit hurried to his side and lifted him.

"You don't seem at all disheartened that someone tried to take my life. That a family member wanted this property so badly he paid to have me killed. That I am nothing but an obstacle for him to overcome. This, the man my mother chose over her son."

"That's how you see this situation?" his spirit asked.

"You don't? My mother allowed her new husband to hire thugs to kill me. Who is the worse snake in the grass? Richard Bonneville, or my mother?"

"You don't know if either of them colluded against you."

"Who else would murder me, then?"

"There could be others." His spirit sat next to him and crossed his arms, tabbing his chin.

"Others? Who? What have I done to anyone else?"

"Nothing that I can think of," the spirit said.

"Are you even capable of thinking?" Grai grunted.

"No. I only read your thoughts. I feel emotions, mostly."

"And yet you don't seem to feel the pain of despair, of hopelessness."

"That sort of pain destroys me, Grai. I do feel hopelessness, but I try to overcome it."

"How? By denying there's a reason for it?"

His spirit shook his head. "Arguing with you is the only way I know how at the moment."

47

Grai sighed. He found no relief in the dispute, and so he dropped the subject.

His spirit sat quietly for a moment, staring at him. Grai could see right through the image. The frosty garden behind him, the fountain, his footprints on the frozen grass. Focusing between his spirit and the holly tree became entertaining. The features in his face took on the pattern of leaves and berries with eyes, a nose, and a mouth.

"What do you have that others might want?" Still, with a perplexed expression on his transparent face, his spirit scratched his head.

"I'm a bachelor living a lonely life in a remote town that few people in this world know about. I'm studying to be an architect. What could anyone want of me, and what harm have I ever done to anyone? You know I have nothing of interest besides my grandfather's estate. You also know my stepfather wants it."

"Ah! But what of all the gold in the root cellar?"

"No one else knows about the gold." He patted his frock wherein the Will nested hidden in his inside pocket.

"Your grandfather had a partner."

"Professor Reinhardt? Yes. But Grandfather insisted his partner was a good man, and his letter states that he already has received his share of the gold."

"Every man is a good man until something triggers their desires, and they see a way of obtaining what they want."

"You think Professor Reinhardt hired someone to kill me?"

His spirit shrugged. Of course, he couldn't think, so that was a silly question to ask him. But his expression encouraged Grai. He stared at the image of a more caring person. A Grai he wished he still had inside of him. A trusting person. His spirit had been the measure of him who wanted to see the world peaceful and beautiful. Just as his spirit turned dead rose buds into colorful blossoms, so too Grai wanted to transform his grandfather's ruins into the oasis it once was. But as each day passed, he came closer to giving up.

"It would be better to think a stranger wanted to kill you than wonder if your family did. That is too devastating a thought for us." his spirit explained.

"I want to know the truth, not pretend that Bonneville didn't hire those men."

"But you don't know the truth," his spirit said. "And until you do, there's no sense in letting your imagination torment you."

"My imagination?" Grai snickered. "You could be my imagination."

His spirit grimaced and nudged him. "I'm not. I'm you. And we have choices right now. There's a future for us—look to that!"

"Future? Is there is a future?" Grai turned away from his spirit. He couldn't think of any future. Not hiding out like he had to do, with an open wound, depending on ice and rain for water, with only the dried rations his grandfather had stored in the root cellars. Oh, there was a wealth of gold in those bags in the dugout, but without the ability to spend it, without being able to show his face in public for fear of being robbed, and not wanting to drag a ghost around with him, his future seemed dim. Death was the only future of which he could conceive.

Grai held his breath and sat up.

"Someone's out there, still," he whispered and nodded toward the wisteria that shrouded the patio garden from where a young woman stood gazing. "Hide me!"

With his spirit lifting him gently from the stone bench, Grai slid under the brush and scooted deep into its mass of twisted branches far enough in the shadows to be hidden, but not so much that he couldn't peek out at the intruder. The movement made his wound bleed again, and so he tightened the wrap and held it in place, wincing. It hurt.

"You'll be okay, Grai," his spirit whispered.

Grai nodded, biting his lip. His spirit took his shoulder and shook him gently. "Hey," he said softly with a smile. "We're going to survive."

Grai doubted anyone could keep on living for long with, of all things, their spirit detached. But he nodded and tried to smile back.

"When we get better," Grai promised, "we're going to find out who our would-be murderers are. The men who took me out, and any man who might have orchestrated the act. I don't think the ones who attacked me did so on their own. They knew what was in my briefcase and ran with all the documents. They thought the Will was in the portfolio. But I don't believe they were common thieves. We're going to find all of them, you and me."

"Yes," his spirit answered eagerly. "Yes, we will."

"They'll come here eventually to claim their spoils. They'll show up. You wait and see."

"We'll watch for them," his spirit answered. "And then what?"

"I'm not sure."

Grai conquered the pain with a deep breath, and with the help of his spirit, he sat upright. He shouldn't be out in the open like this. He should be in the root cellar where he could lock himself away, lie down, and sleep. Too late, he couldn't reach the underground hollow now, even if he could run that far. The woman in the garden would see him.

Grai shuddered, his teeth clattering from the cold and fear. Being almost murdered had not been a joyful experience. He did not want to go through it again. He peeked through the branches and sighed.

"She's only a girl, a teenager," Grai whispered as his spirit settled partly into his body.

He felt a warmth come from the life force's presence, and he relaxed. He would like his spirit to return to him permanently.

"She's not much younger than you, Grai. Look how beautiful she is," his spirit whispered to him.

"Stop that!" Grai responded. "She could be a killer." But she wasn't. He knew it as soon as he saw the softness of her face, her childlike lips, her long lashes touched with frost, her slender figure. Her cheeks had taken on a rosy color that came from cold, and against the dark green of her cloak, she reminded him of a Dutch master's oil painting he'd seen once. His heart softened. That must be his spirit weakening him, and so he nudged it to stop. "Don't be a fool," Grai told him.

"Where are you?" the young woman asked, circling the fountain, glancing at the garden beds. Her skirt brushed against a bench, stirring maple leaves that wavered to the ground. She moved gracefully and had a soft and melodious voice. "I saw you paint the roses. What a stunning display! I would love to talk to you. Please show yourself."

Grai's spirit leaped out of him, and Grai pulled him back.

"Where are you going?"

"She wants us, Grai. She's a friend, I just know she is," his spirit said, delight in his eyes.

"No one is a friend," Grai returned.

"That's not true. You have lots of friends."

"Had, perhaps. Friendships ended the night they stabbed me."

He felt his spirit give in to his will, and that gave Grai the strength to stay hidden. He cowered in the shadow and watched the woman wander around his grandfather's courtyard, touching the wilted flowers. She regarded the ruins with awe and drew in her breath.

"Magnificent," she whispered.

"At least she appreciates our grandfather's work," his spirit whispered.

Grai hoped she wouldn't go near the root cellar. That dugout was his and his alone, and if she got near he'd have to stop her—distract her somehow.

Lost in his thoughts, he didn't realize his spirit had snuck away. Not until a radiance of light touched the fountain did he balk and command the specter back to him. The woman turned suddenly, moving toward where the light had been, but Grai had captured his spirit quickly so that to her, it had vanished.

"You want to speak with her," his spirit begged.

"No, I don't. Why would I?"

"She's beautiful."

"True enough. I'm happy to sit here in the shadows and watch her." Indeed, seeing another human being as lovely as this woman satisfied his loneliness for the moment. He had no desire to speak to her. What Grai wanted was to have control over his spirit! Oh, how he wished to be lighthearted again, yes, but with common sense. Until they were one—if that were at all possible—he would hide like a deer in the woods.

"Then let me get her closer to you so you can see the glimmer in her eyes," his spirit urged. "She is truly a jewel."

"And if she sees us?" Grai asked.

"What's to lose?"

"My life."

"She won't hurt you," his spirit pled.

"She'll talk. All women talk. They cannot discover me. It's bad enough she saw you in this condition. What do you suppose she thinks? That we're ghosts!"

"Foolishness. She'd fall in love with us."

"You're the fool," Grai growled softly. "This estate is our only refuge. We have nowhere else to go, nor do we have a choice but to get well. After that, we can find the assailants before they kill me. And you had better believe we will confront Richard Bonneville before I die. Can you rationalize thrusting this lovely young lady into our efforts? She could get hurt. I thought you were the compassionate one?"

"You need to meet her," his spirit said. "She's come to help you."

Grai watched her. As vitalizing as the elusive hues of roses from hoarfrost, this young woman anointed the skeleton of his grandfather's estate with a fragrance of life he would like to breathe for an exceedingly long time.

Winter Vision

Adele returned to the gate and waited within the shadows, monitoring Benjamin as he wandered about the garden beds on her uncle's property, weighed down in his heavy coat, his scarf pulled up to his ears, and his breath a puff of steam as he searched.

"Adele!" he called.

Moving further under the honeysuckle, she considered hiding as she'd be a fool to acknowledge him. It would be even more foolish to stay by this fence where he could find her. She stealthily slid away into the neighbor's yard and remained in the ruins until Benjamin went back in the house. She sighed, disappointed that she couldn't go home and stand by the fire yet. The cold had found its way through her coat, her toes were frozen, her ears numb, her nose runny, and certainly her cheeks were bright red. The sky had grown heavier and flakes of snow fell. She wandered back onto the patio and surveyed the ruins that had initially lured her.

Despite the wintriness, lingering a while longer in this paradise was not a complete sacrifice. The charm of these private grounds soothed her discomfort, and she soon imagined how this mansion might have appeared before the fire and the earthquake. Judging from the size of the courtyard, the house had been much grander than her uncle's manor. The foundation suggested that the home had been colossal, with marble pillars at its entrance. Those pillars had toppled and broken into pieces, now rubble strewed and scattered about the courtyard. How many stories had the mansion been? And had the ivy crawled to the top of the towers? Were there cathedral ceilings inside? Were the walls and floor covered with ceramic tile? And did roses, irises, lavender, and foxgloves grow in these beds?

Adele had never seen a more handsome piece of artwork as the fountain's statue standing in front of her. A Grecian gown flowed over her smooth alabaster arms, her molded eyes looked gently at a pool where fish might have swum. The moss gave the figure color and character. The sculpture water jug, glossy, must have once released a stream of water. Behind the statue, covered with rust, was an iron tank and a hand pump. She tried to work the pump, but of course, both the pump and any water in the tank had been frozen. Her gloves stuck to the handle, and she pulled them free.

Adele surveyed the courtyard again, hoping to see the apparition. She would like to communicate with him. The look on his face had given her chills as if he had human intelligence and had been scrutinizing her in the same manner she had been examining him. He wasn't at all like the ghosts she read about. Vaporous and wild, oblivious to reality. This ghost was young and handsome. He wasn't the spirit of an old man who died. But who was he? Did he dwell in the graveyard? How did he die? Was he a troubled spirit hoping to find his way to the Afterlife? Her mother had told her stories about troubled ghosts—that they dallied near humans until they found a medium to send them on to the next world.

Adele walked again to the bed of roses. Leafless, what blackened buds remained were dead. Yet these were the same roses that the phantom had touched and kindled to life, making them rich with color just moments before. She had never heard of ghosts performing miracles as he did.

He might not be a ghost. He might be an angel.

Her curiosity unsettled her the same as a hunger needing to satisfy. She'd always believed in the supernatural. The days she spent alone as a child had heightened her imagination. The enchanting tales her father told her when she was a little girl emboldened her dreams. She wanted to believe in the mystical and here was her opportunity for discovery!

The clouds gathered overhead, dark, and dangerous, and even more sizable snowflakes fell, now. She couldn't stay much longer. Aunt Eloise would worry and come looking for her, and Adele didn't want them to find her here. She would keep the miracle of the phantom to herself. She turned once again to leave, but a wishing well camouflaged by moss and deadened vines caught her attention. A wooden bucket dangled on a rope over the center of the red-brick wishing well, and when she leaned over and looked down, the sight surprised her.

"Someone's been making wishes!" she laughed. Gold coins shimmered under a layer of ice, bright, shiny, and newly minted. Odd, but someone must have tossed these in here recently.

A current of warm air swept across her cheeks, and when she looked up, there he was. The phantom, his eyes stayed on her.

They were hazel, and he had a fragrance about him, not sweet like women's perfume, but akin to cedar or evergreen. When he moved, the sunlight caught the color of his clothing, a gray coat, a soiled shirt that might have been white once, dark trousers that had a blue hue, all translucent so that she could see through him.

Though she shivered from the chill, perspiration trickle down her brow and sweat coagulated on her palms inside her mittens. She meandered around the well, her mind racing. "Please," she said softly with the sweetest voice she could manage despite her fear.

"Please talk to me. Please tell me who you are and why you're here."

In the same way that she approached him, the spirit retreated. Gradually luring her away, floating backward, his eyes fixed on her with a pleasant, friendly expression. She passed by the fountain one step at a time, speaking gently.

"Are you in some sifting of trouble? Is there a way I can help you? Do you even speak? Do you have a name? Are you lost?"

Whether the spirit could communicate, she didn't know, but she kept asking him questions, regardless. She would try to strike a chord with him and provoke him into answering her. All she wanted was a conversation so she could discover more about him. She followed across the courtyard at turtle's pace until she understood he was leading her to another part of the garden she had not yet explored. Latticework in need of paint supported a huge vine that extended from the courtyard to a patio beyond.

Her fear returned, and she slowed, ceasing her interrogation. Where was he leading her?

The spirit retreated even farther after she stopped, and she saw that he had drawn her to a young man leaning against the arbor. Once the spirit met up with him, it vanished into him, and yet there were hints of his presence flickering in and around him. She couldn't focus on the man entirely, it was as though she were seeing double. She blinked several times, but the illusion would not go away.

Adele lost her breath, so unorthodox was this encounter. The man's eyes stayed fixed on her, not once acknowledging the phantom. He looked exactly like the vision—curly hair matted and tangled, a sandy color that shimmered with red highlights in the sunlight. He wore a tailored frock over his shoulders. His shirt hung loose and open, and he had a bandage wrapped around his torso which leaked blood. She gasped, for the wound looked fresh and vile, and he appeared pale as if dead.

"Are you a ghost?" she asked, the words barely escaping her lips.

"You see?" the man said with difficulty, though he didn't seem to be speaking to her. "What did I tell you?" He said nothing else, and so Adele stepped closer.

"You're hurt."

He stood as still as the figure in the fountain.

"Can I help you? Or…," she swallowed. "Or are you dead?"

"I'm not dead," he whispered.

That was good to know! She ceased from getting too near him.

"My name is Adele Johansson. I live with my uncle next door."

She thought he'd introduce himself as well, but he didn't. He only stared at her with gentle eyes, his lids half open and his lips chapped and parted. Sweat dripped down his brow, and she could tell he was in pain. He wasn't dead, but in this cold weather and with that wound, and that flickering spirit-thing moving in and out of him, he may be close to it.

"Let me help you," she said again, having no means of helping him.

"He could use your help," the phantom moved out of him and spoke. "His name is Grai, and he's shy. But I can speak for him."

"Oh?" Adele stepped back. This was the strangest situation she'd ever been in, speaking to a man and his spirit disjointedly.

"You should come home with me. My aunt and I will get medical care for you," she offered, not certain of the reception her aunt and uncle would give. The situation looked suspicious—a dying man loitering in the ruins of their neighbor's property could easily cause alarm.

"My aunt and uncle are good people. They can take care of you."

"No!" Grai snapped.

"He…he's hiding, Adele. No one should see him like this."

"Hiding?"

Grai frowned at the spirit and it wavered around him and then into him once more so that she saw double again. She blinked, trying to focus.

"Are you wanted by the law?" she asked.

"No," Grai answered. "The spirit thinks he can speak for me, but don't listen to him. There are reasons I can't be seen. I have committed no crime, though. I need to rest, and I would ask that you leave," Grai told her. "Please. Just go back to where you came from and say nothing. I didn't mean for you to see me. It was all his idea."

"You're hurt."

"I can manage it."

"If you'd let me tell my aunt, I'm sure she knows a physician."

"No physician. No aunt."

The spirit grunted, sprouted away, and circled behind Grai, who leaned on the arbor, weak and hurting and with no one to help him. What could Adele do? She had no herbs, no wraps for his wound, not even a cup of tea or hot cocoa to warm his belly.

"Grai, sir," Adele said, reaching out but afraid to touch him. "I will leave you to your rest. But I'm returning with medicine and maybe warm blankets, so you don't have to be cold. I won't say a word to anyone. Trust me."

"No..." he drew a breath and rolled his eyes. He looked as though he were going to die right there and then. Adele gasped and put her hand over her mouth as Grai slid to the ground.

She knelt next to him and the spirit appeared by her side.

"Please, get your medicine," he said. "I'll take him inside. Please come back."

"Yes. I'll return as soon as I can." She didn't want to, but she left him there. Looking back over her shoulder, she saw the spirit lift Grai to his feet and, with the man leaning heavily on the apparition, walk him away from the garden. To where, she couldn't tell.

Adele hurried over the icy courtyard and onto the vine-covered trail leading to the postern. Once she had a view of Uncle Nicholas' driveway and saw that Benjamin's coach had left, she pushed open the gate and latched it shut. Snowfall came steady and thick, covering her woolen scarf and coat and sticking to the ground. Her boots squeaked as she plodded by the garden beds.

The confrontation with Grai motivated her. He mustn't die, not now that she knew about him and could help him. She would do everything she could. There had to be a medicine bag somewhere in Aunt Eloise's possession. Even her mother kept clean cotton wraps and camphor and other herbs in case of cuts. She had promised not to tell anyone about him, even though she wondered why. Still, his affairs were his own. Knowing that he had an injury made her responsible to come to his aide.

Once she arrived at the manor, she gathered an armload of firewood, opened the door with one hand, and stomped the frost and snow off her boots. Heat still radiated from the cookstove, but the fire had been snuffed. The dishes had been cleaned, the cast iron hung on the wall, the icebox polished, and plates placed carefully in the china cabinet. The family had eaten supper, and she missed it.

She stepped into the living room, firewood still piled in her arms, and halted. Uncle Nicholas stood by the hearth and lifted his chin when their eyes met. He wore his red silk smoking jacket that reeked of tobacco, but he held no pipe. Aunt Eloise dressed for town in her bustle gown had her hands folded and sat facing him on the davenport. Maggie rested on the braided rug in front of the fire with Butterscotch on her lap, and Peter, in the rocking chair, turned pages to a book. The monotonous squeak of his rocker interrupted the otherwise stiff silence. The boy snickered when Adele glanced at him. The children's parents were nowhere to be seen.

"And where have you been, Miss Johansson?" Uncle Nicholas asked, his voice gruff and stern, his eyes dark and piercing.

"I was…," Adele began. She regarded her aunt. The woman's eyes were red, and she held a hankie. "I was getting firewood."

"You left to get firewood two hours ago."

"Have I been gone that long?" She avoided her uncle's eyes.

"You missed supper, Adele," her aunt said meekly. "Benjamin went to fetch you and he couldn't find you anywhere."

"I'm sorry."

"Where were you?" The tone in her uncle's voice frightened her. Rarely had she been spoken to in such an authoritative tone. "Put that measly pile of wood in the rack and sit on the couch next to your aunt. I have a few words for you."

"Sorry, sir," Adele knelt at the wood rack and stacked the few logs she had brought in one upon the other, her thoughts spinning. She needed to return to Grai with medicine. He might die if she didn't go quickly, but how would she escape this predicament?

"For as many hours that you were gone, you'd think you'd have brought in an entire forest. Hurry!" Uncle Nicholas commanded so sharply she jumped up and dropped the last chunk of wood on the floor. Wood chips scattered off her skirt and gloves. Her heart raced as she picked up the wood that fell and placed it on the rack.

He pointed to the couch.

"You are under our charge and God knows we have neither the time nor energy to follow you around with a cane, herding you like a pet pig."

"Nicholas!" Aunt Eloise interrupted.

"Hush woman! I'm talking. I'll get to you in a moment. This is a warning for you, Adele. One more mishap like this and I will use my belt."

"Nicholas, she's not a child. She's too old to whip," Aunt Eloise declared.

"She's not too old for discipline. Obviously, your sister spent so much time in criminal activity she failed to teach her daughter manners. If we don't set this child on the road to civility, she may find herself at the end of a noose like her parents."

Adele whimpered and covered her mouth. Must he be such a brute? Aunt Eloise took her hand and squeezed it.

"What? Does that upset you?" he asked Adele.

"Of course, it upsets her." Aunt Eloise protested, springing off the couch. "Do you think she needs constant reminders of her mother and father's fate? Stop this badgering, Nick. There's no reason to be so heartless!"

Uncle Nicholas raised an eyebrow and stared at his wife. "Really? And you would demean my discipline, Eloise?"

"What you're doing isn't discipline, it's brutality. She's defenseless and I'm going to speak on her behalf as long as you're a beast. I won't have you treating her like one of your horses. We need to encourage her, not condemn her."

Uncle Nicholas folded his arms across his chest. His dark eyes pinned Adele to the couch and his face turned red.

"We should treat her as a part of this family. She needs room to grow, to explore."

He winced at that word. "Explore what?"

"Everything, Nicholas. This environment is unfamiliar to her, the home, the grounds, the town. A world has opened up to her, and she wants to see it. She needs to see it if she's going to flourish as a modern woman."

"Modern woman?" Uncle Nicholas snickered. "More of your insubordination talking."

"Must we discuss this again, Nicholas? I'm your partner in life. They freed slaves in America if I remember correctly."

"Are you insinuating that I enslave you?"

"Not at all. And you shall not. Nor shall you enslave Adele. She's a healthy young lady who is ripe to learn everything we can teach her."

"And how do you suggest we do that? Just let her wander around aimlessly in the woods as she's been doing?" he emphasized that word so dramatically that Adele looked up at him. Did he know where she'd been? Did that upset him?

"Give me a chance to take Adele under my wing. I promise she'll be more punctual. Isn't that right, Adele?"

"Yes, I promise I will be more responsible than I have been," Adele muttered. *Just please let me get back to Grai.*

"I'll take her shopping this afternoon when I go with Lila. Adele has nothing formal to wear at the reception, and Josephine's Mercantile just had a shipment of fabric arrive."

"You'll take her nowhere in town. Not unless I'm there with you. There is too much talk about the hanging. She's not safe in public at the moment. Let the rumors subside before we present Adele to Port Summerhill. I know those people. They'll scorn her, or worse. Adele can prove herself trustworthy by minding our grandchildren while you take Lila to town."

Adele glanced out the window. *Perhaps he'll be all right, even if I don't return tonight.*

"And Eloise, if you think you can do something with her, she's your charge. Should she error like this again, I will punish the both of you!" With that, the man strode to the foyer, grabbed his coat and his hat from the coat rack, and walked out the door. A hush swept over the room after he left, and for the first time, Adele noticed Peter staring at her with a scornful smile. Lila stood in the hall, exchanging a glance with her mother.

"Well, I'm glad that's over with and no casualties! You were fortunate, Adele," her cousin stated. "Father's been a lot rougher for a lot less."

"Why was he so angry?" Adele asked.

"Nicholas insists on running a tight household. I'm sorry you hadn't been warned, but everyone is expected to be at the table when called for dinner. I should prepare you a list of guidelines in the future."

"Guidelines titled *How not to make Uncle Nicholas Angry*, yes I think I could use something like that."

"Watching your mouth might be a good place to start," Lila informed her.

"Adele, we'll have a talk when I get home. Lila, are you ready?" Aunt Eloise brushed the wrinkles out of her bustle and buttoned her waistcoat. "I'm sorry you can't come, Adele. Perhaps you and the children will enjoy each other's company. Peter's particularly good at chess and as long as Maggie has Butterscotch, I don't think you'll find any complaints from her."

Adele glanced at Maggie. The girl was in another world conversing with the cat, holding the animal's head in her little hands and kissing its nose. Peter pretended to be reading his book, but the smirk on his face hadn't disappeared.

Adele saw her aunt and cousin out and closed the door, feeling a bit awkward with the children and anxious about Grai. He said they were going to rest, so he must have a place to lie down out of the cold. She hoped.

The children occupied themselves for a time, Peter reading and Maggie playing with the cat. Adele paced by the window, contemplating how she might help Grai and watch the children simultaneously when she jumped, startled by Butterscotch's hiss. Adele turned around sharply just as the cat backed out of Maggie's hands and raced under a chair. Maggie screamed.

"Leave her be," Peter said. "She tires of you harassing her."

Maggie sneered at Peter. "I wasn't havasting her. I was petting

64

her."

"You were pulling her ears. Cat's don't like that."

"She likes me. She likes everything I do," Maggie jumped up, holding a fist up in the air and shaking it at her brother.

"She hates you, Maggie. Just admit it."

"Children, please," Adele interrupted. "You never argue when your grandparents are around. Why do it now?"

"We argue, they just don't hear it," Peter said and closed his book.

"Well, I don't want to hear the fussing, either." Adele stated.

Peter popped his cheek with this thumb in defiance. A lock from his blond hair fell over his eyes, and he curled his nose at her.

"We don't care what you want. You're from the ghetto town."

Heat soared to Adele's cheeks. She wondered what sort of things Benjamin said to Peter in private.

"Don't speak to me in that tone, young man," she said.

Peter laughed. "What are you going to do to stop me? You can't touch me, or I'll tell my mother and make life miserable for you."

Adele stared at him, aghast. Not only did he look like her cousin, but he also sounded just like him.

She took a deep breath and peered out the window.

"What say we go outside and make a snowman?"

"Yes!" Maggie clapped her hands and ran for her coat in the foyer.

"I'd rather throw snowballs at Magdalene," Peter said. "And you. I will pop you in the head with one."

"Oh, really? We'll see how far that gets you!" Adele dared him.

A snowball fight might get him out of his mood, though she'd love to just stuff his mouth with snow.

After she had them in their coats and boots, mittens and warm hats tied tightly around their ears, Adele guided them out the door. Their feet sank a good three inches in the snow and both Peter and Maggie, thrilled at making the first footprints stomped, jumped, and slid into the front yard, throwing themselves at the banks of snow that piled up around the huckleberry bushes. Maggie rolled in powder and made a snow angel while Peter made the first snowball and tossed it gently at his sister. She screamed, laughed, and then grabbed a handful of snow and threw it at him. He dodged away and made another snowball, but this one landed on the side of Adele's head. Adele reciprocated, catching him by his collar and tucking a pile of snow down the back of his neck. He screamed and laughed, and for that, Adele sighed in relief. She did not want to be enemies with Lila's little boy. They played rough and Adele had her share of snow to eat, but the sport was worthy and fun for the three of them.

"Let's build a snowman," Adele said after falling, breathless. She and Peter rolled a ball of snow to the size of a boulder, letting it stand in the middle of the patio. Peter piled a second ball on top and Adele made the head. From there Adele kept a watchful eye on the neighbor's property as they worked, hoping Aunt Eloise and Lila would return before dark so she could keep her word to Grai.

The short winter day dimmed well before it should have, and still, the women did not return home. The snowman had fallen apart several times before Adele could get his face on, but when there was a nice smooth ball for a head fixed on his sloping shoulders, Peter went inside to find a carrot to use as a nose, and Maggie found two leaves for his eyes. Just as Maggie handed the second leaf to Adele, the screen door slammed, and Peter screamed. He pointed toward the neighbor's yard.

Maggie jumped up and let out an ear-piercing screech before Adele saw the object of their horror. The little girl's face brightened, and tears fell from the corner of her eyes.

"Mama!" she cried.

To Adele's horror, Grai's spirit stood by the fence.

"Oh, no!" Adele whispered. She didn't need to tell the children to run into the house, they had already fled. Maggie slipped on the way and bruised her knee. Adele's heart pounded not with fear but with anger as she picked the child up and rushed to the door. How foolish to have exposed himself! But then, she realized he was waiting for her to keep her promise and return with medicine. Grai needed her care. And soon.

The Medicine Bag

Peter clammed up once in the house, but Maggie kept crying. Adele made them both change out of their wet clothes and washed them with warm water, put their chemises on, and tucked them in bed. Neither of the children complained about retiring before their mother returned. By the looks in their eyes, they were exhausted and horrified both. Adele read a story to them and her quiet voice put Maggie to sleep. Peter simply listened and stared at the ceiling. It would be to Adele's benefit if the children would forget their trauma and not speak of the ghost they saw, at least not until they were home, and their parents were the only ones who heard their story. Uncle Nicholas would be livid at her if he thought Adele had subjected his grandchildren to danger. He seemed to enjoy being angry with her. With any luck, Lila and her husband would count the experience as nothing more than a wild fantasy.

While Peter and Maggie slept soundly in the guest room, tucked under a downy quilt, Adele searched every closet she could comfortably access without feeling like a burglar. If a medicine bag of some sort existed in this household, it would be hidden or sealed in a vault. She searched every armoire, every dark corner, and under every bed but could not find it. If she simply asked Aunt Eloise when she came home, the woman would be suspicious. Even inquiring with Mei Ling could cause alarm, though Mei Ling had already retired to her bunkhouse.

She put another log on the fire as the cold night air brought a chill into the house. Poor Grai must be frozen out there. She couldn't leave, not with the children under her charge, but she did manage to set aside two blankets from off of her bed. She could wrap herself in a coat to stay warm at night if she had to. Or curl up next to Butterscotch. Grai didn't have that luxury.

She delved into the kitchen cupboards and filled a knapsack with jerky, a loaf of bread, cheese, and nuts. There was plenty of food to bring him, and he would be grateful she was sure. But after stuffing her pack full she regarded it all as trivial. Bringing Grai blankets and food would not save his life.

He needed medicine.

His wound should be wrapped with a poultice, clean gauze, sulfur, or camphor to protect the lesion from infection. She'd seen the doctor in Port Galleon treat oyster harvesters who had accidents at work. Always a salve was applied to the wound and wrapped tightly. How could her aunt and uncle not have medical supplies? Even her parents kept a collection of herbs.

While in the kitchen she heard the carriage arrive and her aunt and uncle laughing. The lantern in the foyer flickered when the door opened, and shadows were cast against the wainscoting as they stomped the snow off their boots and hung their coats on the coat rack. Snow fell onto the floor as Uncle Nicholas shook his top hat.

To avoid any suspicion, Adele had tucked the knapsack in the potato draw. She could retrieve that on her way out the door. She pulled out a round of cheese from the pantry coated in wax. Above the counter hung Mei Ling's knife collection—many impressive blades sharp and glistening in the lantern light. Adele chose the largest and held it over the cheese, biting her lip, preparing herself. When Aunt Eloise and Lila came into the living room with bundles of packages in their arms, Adele rolled up her sleeve and pushed the knife into her arm. Blood trickled out of her body and she screamed, dropped the knife, and ran to them, holding her hand over the wound, blood dripping onto her skirt and leaving a trail on the floor.

"Help! Help me!" she cried. Auntie dropped her packages on the davenport and ran to her. Uncle Nicholas raced down the hall. Lila rushed to the kitchen and saturated a tea towel with water.

Adele kept screaming and her vision blurred from the hysteria, but she blinked away the tears, watching carefully as the family gathered around her. She paid special attention to Uncle Nicholas as he brought a black leather bag from the den. Aunt Eloise held Adele's arm while Uncle Nicholas quickly unlatched the bag, pulled out a vial, and poured a portion of the contents onto a cloth.

"Don't use it all," Adele gasped. He frowned.

"I'll use as much as I need to, young lady," he said as he released another drop from the vial. He wrapped the cloth around her arm and tied the bandage with a thin strip of leather to secure it in place.

"Keep your arm elevated. Above your heart. It will slow the bleeding. What were you doing with a knife?" Aunt Eloise asked.

"I was hungry. I was trying to get a piece of cheese."

"I knew we were gone too long, mother," Lila complained. "Where are Peter and Maggie?"

"In bed. They're fine. Don't wake them up." Adele panicked. "Let them sleep!"

"I must wake them if I'm to get them home," Lila said and took her leave to the guest room.

"There! That should stop the bleeding," Uncle Nicholas huffed as he tightened the knot. "But I doubt it will stop the insanity." He stepped back, put the vial back in the bag, and latched it shut.

"Where are you taking that?" Adele asked.

He furrowed his brow. "I'm putting it back in the den where it belongs. Why?"

"Just in case I bleed through this wrap in the middle of the night, I wouldn't want to wake you."

"That's very kind of you to think of our feelings, but your aunt and I will see to it you're taken care of," he answered and took his medicine bag back down the hall. She watched with an eagle eye and could see the mirror in the den, and his reflection as he tucked the bag into the armoire. She sighed, calculating her next move. It couldn't be tonight, not with everyone giving her so much attention—in the morning, early.

#

Adele woke after sleeping under the warmth of her wool coat. She hadn't yet brought her blankets to Grai, but she slept without them to make sure she'd be comfortable enough. Butterscotch kept her warm, warmer than that poor man suffering outside by himself. She could talk Aunt Eloise into letting him stay in one of the guest rooms. She promised him she wouldn't say anything though, so she'd have to persuade him first. To do that she'd have to convince him she was sincere. And to do that she'd have to keep her word.

"I'm afraid they may be doubting me already!" she told Butterscotch. "I should have been there last night."

She scooted the cat aside and crawled out of bed, immediately reminded of the cut on her arm. Her wound had bled through the thin cotton dressing and needed another gauze. *Good! That gives me a valid reason to access the bag of supplies.*

Adele slipped her robe over her nightgown and crept downstairs expecting everyone to be asleep, but Aunt Eloise moved about in the parlor unpacking the bundles that had been brought home from town the night before.

"Adele! You're up early. Shouldn't you be dressed before coming down here?"

"My arm is bleeding again, and I didn't want to stain my clothes."

"Let me see." Aunt Eloise set down the package and held out her hand. When Adele showed her the wound, she pouted "Let's get that changed."

"I can get the bag if you want. I could probably even change the dressing myself if you're too busy."

"Nonsense, I'm not too busy for my favorite niece." Her smile sent a chill through Adele. Favorite niece? Not that Aunt Eloise had any other nieces, but still, Adele hadn't received affection from family for a long while. She blushed, taken aback by those simple words. Adele, in her selfishness, hadn't taken the time to see that Aunt Eloise truly did care about her.

The woman slipped out of the parlor, leaving Adele in front of a pile of pale green fabric. Silk? Shiny and smooth, the fabric glistened with an array of colors so that it wasn't just green but had shades of blue and yellow and even silver where sunlight shone on it. She wanted to touch it but dared not with her arm bleeding.

"Ah! I see you found your dress," Aunt Eloise said when she returned and set the bag next to the material.

"My dress?"

"Well, it's not put together yet, but soon. I work fairly quickly, and we have plenty of time. We fitted the bodice to Lila in your stead, but you two are remarkably similar in size and I can adjust it if I need to. Let's get your arm wrapped better than Nicholas' attempt last night. When that's done, I'd like you to model for me this morning so I can pin the fabric."

"I..." Adele hesitated. She needed to tend to Grai, but she couldn't tell Aunt Eloise. "How long will it take?"

"Oh, I imagine I'll be finished before too long. You're not in a hurry for any reason, are you?" Auntie had meant that in humor.

"No—."

Aunt Eloise had already taken the soiled dressing off Adele's arm, folded it carefully, and placed it in a wastebasket. She opened a jar of salve, took two fingers fully, and applied it to her arm.

"This is not that deep of a cut. I think you were most frightened," she said. "Some girls faint at the sight of blood. You did well."

"What's that you're using?"

"Camphor and mullein leaves. The camphor will keep infection away and mullein will draw out any infection that might already have gained hold." She tightened the lid and returned it to the bag. Aunt Eloise wrapped the bandage around more securely than Uncle Nicholas had. "I don't think it will bleed again so you needn't worry about it soiling your clothes. Hustle now and get dressed. Then come back here so I can work on your gown."

Adele had no choice but to return, and all this time meant Grai would suffer. After changing her clothes, she hurried back to her aunt. Every moment that passed would be a mark against her promise. Every hour, a stain against her integrity. Would he even live that long?

Aunt Eloise unpacked the bodice and held it up for her to see.

"It's so different!" Adele exclaimed.

"It's the new fashion. They call the bodice the Princess. It's the same cut Alexandra Princess of Wales wears. She's a fashion queen all over the world now. You, my dear, get to debut this style in Port Summerhill."

As Adele stood on a stool garbed in the elegant satin and lace bodice Aunt Eloise pinned layers and layers of silk around her. Adele sweated and prayed. If, when she finally gets to Grai, she finds him dead, she'll never forgive herself.

"You haven't even asked about this gala that we're attending next week," her aunt stated.

"I wasn't sure what to ask," Adele said.

"Well," Aunt Eloise took a pin out of her mouth and pushed it through a fold at the hem. "Your uncle and his colleagues have invited several important bankers and railroad men from San Francisco to the hotel. They're going to present their final proposal for the railroad. If they can convince these men that our town is a key city for the west, Nicholas says it will put us on the map!"

"What does that mean for us?" Adele asked, hoping her question sounded intelligent.

"What it means is Nicholas will soon be doing a lot of investing."

"Investing?"

"He plans on buying more property. He'll start with the acreage that adjoins our estate and move on from there."

Adele's eyes widened. What a curious change of events. She wasn't sure why the prospect of her uncle buying that property sat ill with her other than if he finds Grai and thinks he's a trespasser or a criminal he might act against him. Then again, he might not want anything to do with the property when he discovers a ghost lives there. Adele planned on unraveling the mystery of Grai's presence herself. If Uncle Nicholas called the marshal and had him arrested as a vagabond, she would never forgive herself.

"Once a railway comes through here, the town will expand, and any investments will multiply in value. It's extremely exciting. Something your uncle has been dreaming of for a long time."

"I thought you were already wealthy."

She laughed and stood, setting the rest of the pins in her sewing basket. "We're more in debt than we are wealthy. The whole town is in debt. We need the railroad, and so this meeting is extremely important." She smiled at Adele. "And you will be absolutely stunning. There may even be a young fellow or two at this gala who will catch your eye."

Adele blushed. "But my reputation won't be pleasing for any of these young fellows," she reminded her aunt.

"You have no reputation. What your parents did is not what you did. Don't let it follow you."

Adele looked in the mirror that Aunt Eloise held up for her. She had never worn a dress made with silk and lace before. All she had ever worn were earthy colors, wool, and cotton. This dress had style, a gown that only wealthy women wore.

"I don't know what to say, Auntie. It's beautiful and I love the color."

"It does well on you. Lila chose the fabric. Now. Let's get you out of this. With your uncle in Port Summerhill all day, I want to use the time to sew."

"Uncle Nicholas is leaving for the day?"

"He's making preparations for next week."

What an extremely fortunate turn of events. With Aunt Eloise busy sewing, and Uncle Nicholas away, Adele could take the medicine and blankets and what bit of food she packed away to Grai without worry. She dressed hurriedly and once in her drab, woolen clothes again; she eyed the medicine bag on the floor.

"I'll put this bag back in the den for you," she suggested.

"Thank you," her aunt said, preoccupied with fitting the bodice on a mannequin.

Adele picked up the medicine bag, slipped out of the room, and quietly shut the parlor door. Speeding up the stairs to the tower, she fetched the blankets and tiptoed back down. Mei Ling had not yet awakened to fix breakfast, so getting the knapsack she had left in the kitchen was effortless. After bundling herself for winter weather, she dodged out the back door.

Grai and Adele

No one told her Benjamin would be shoveling snow from the cellar steps on the west side of the house. Seeing him caused her to draw her breath and come to a standstill by the kitchen door. She threw the blankets over the medicine bag and tucked the bundle tightly under her arm. Before she stepped into the open, she eyed him and then looked away. He saw her, and of all the rude things for him to do, he whistled.

"Hey sweetheart," he called and stuck his shovel upright in the snow.

Adele froze contemplating on what sort of reception to give him. She could keep walking and ignore him hoping he didn't pursue her, but where would she go with Benjamin following her? No! Better to divert him somehow. She would stand up to him and let him know she's not afraid of him.

"What do you want Benjamin?" she asked.

"You know what I want," he laughed as he strolled casually over the path he'd shoveled earlier. He wore his scarf high on his neck and his cap low. His blue eyes a vivid contrast against his rosy cheeks.

"Please, Benjamin, stop this. You know I have nothing for you."

He touched her hair, and she jerked and pushed his arm away with her free hand.

"Why don't you leave me alone? I've done nothing to you to deserve your offensives. I haven't even tattled on you for the last time you accosted me."

He laughed again. "You're so pretty when you're mad. Where are you going?"

"I thought I'd sit in the garden and have a picnic," she answered.

"In the snow?"

"Yes. In the snow." Adele stepped out of the shade, eyeing one of the many garden benches steaming in the sunshine.

"May I join you?"

"No. You're not done with your chores."

"I have a more important chore to do." He drew far too close to her, his breath warming her neck. Even though Benjamin was tall and lanky, he was strong, and he used his strength to push Adele up against the side of the house. His lips were on hers before she knew what happened. Her heart raced more out of anger than fear. She bit his lip, kneed him in the groin, and dodged under his arm. The blankets trailed her in the snow, but she clenched the bag tightly in her hands.

Aunt Eloise called Benjamin before Adele got to the edge of the garden and when she turned around he was gone, having slipped into the house through the kitchen door.

Adele waited, her heart thumping. She scanned the windows of the manor to see if she were being watched. There was no sign of anyone either upstairs or in the kitchen. Satisfied that she was alone, she backed up to the gate and then hurriedly darted through it.

Once camouflaged from view by the honeysuckle vines on the other side of the fence, she dropped the bag, the blankets, and her scarf, and leaned against the vines to catch her breath.

"He's a lover of yours?"

Grai stood a few feet from her. He looked healthier today, or perhaps because the sun shone on his curls, and his hazel eyes sparkled in the light.

"No! I wish he would leave me alone. He's a cousin. A rude one."

Grai frowned and looked past her toward her uncle's property.

"That's not right. He shouldn't be treating you in such an ill manner."

"It's very wrong but I don't know how to escape him."

"Does he live there?"

"No. He lives with his sister. But he spends time helping his parents do repairs on the house. I can't avoid him."

She did not mean to upset Grai by complaining about Benjamin so when he grimaced and continued eyeing her uncle's garden, she held out her gifts to him.

"I brought you some blankets so you don't have to freeze at night. And I have medicine for your wound. Please let me dress it. I went through a lot to get these items to you."

"You didn't tell anyone about me, did you?"

"Heavens no!"

He glanced past her toward her uncle's house again and then nodded. Without another word, he led her to the courtyard. His spirit shimmered in and out of him and then peeked over his shoulder at her, smiled, and winked. She couldn't help but smile back. The spirit's influence seemed to make Grai more accepting of her and had a way of putting her at ease. Her shoulders relaxed and her gait slowed.

The pools of the fountain had been cleaned of leaves and ice and now a cascade of sparkling water splashed out of the statue's jug and swirled about in ripples that reflected the blue of the sky.

"It's beautiful!" she exclaimed. Grai turned and stopped as she admired the fountain and his spirit slipped away from him.

"You fixed it! It's working! It's so pretty!"

"All for you my fair lady!" Grai's spirit said. They both looked at Grai. He walked away from them.

"It must have been difficult to get it to work!"

"He fixed it this morning. I cautioned him about his wound, but

78

he wanted to have the waterfall working for you before you returned."

"For me?"

"He said ladies love fountains."

"Nonsense," Grai argued and waved the thought away. "I fixed it for the birds that they might have water to drink."

Grai sat on the bench across from the fountain, removed his wool scarf, his coat, his shirt, and proceeded to unwrap the soiled rag that covered his wound. Adele hurried to his side, removed her coat to work more freely, and threw it on the bench with the blankets.

"It's very noble of you caring for the birds, but you should be taking better care of this wound so that it doesn't fester," she scolded.

A ghastly sight, the cut had obviously been made with a very sharp knife or dagger and it was deep. Rolling up her sleeves so as not to get them wet, Adele dipped the cloth in the fountain, and with the ointment her uncle had used on her, she cleaned his injury by dabbing the dried blood away with a gentle touch.

Grai winced but didn't back away or cry out. His spirit leaned over her and watched intently as she worked, letting out grunts and groans in sympathy until Grai scowled at him.

Once the wound had been cleansed, Adele opened the bottle of herbs that Aunt Eloise used on her that morning, scooped out a large swab, and applied it generously over the cut. Grai recoiled, flinching when she packed the lesion, but he stayed strong and let her finish. She unrolled the cotton dressing from the medicine bag, unrolled it, and reached around him to wrap his torso with the bandage. She felt his eyes on her as she touched him. She tucked the end neatly onto itself to secure it. When she was done, he took her arm and gently touched the bandage her aunt had applied that morning.

"What happened here?"

"Just a cut."

"How so?"

"I didn't know where this medicine bag was and there was only one way to find out without being accused of thievery or having someone follow me."

His mouth fell open. "You cut yourself on my behalf?"

"It's just a little scratch."

"Why? Why would you do something like that for a stranger?"

"I don't know, I wanted to help." Heat rushed to her cheeks. She shouldn't have told him. "It's wrong for you to be here all by yourself with a terrible wound. Who do you have to help you? No one. I found you here, and so now it is my responsibility to take care of you." She brushed her hands on her skirt. "There. I'm not sure how well that will stay."

"It'll stay," he said, amazement in his eyes.

"Do you mind if I ask what happened to you?" Carefully rolling the loose gauze, stalling for time for she didn't want to leave, she packed away her potions.

Grai's spirit gave Grai an eager nod, prompting a grimace from him.

"I was…assaulted," Grai said. "I can't believe you cut yourself on my behalf."

"Think little of it. Please. It doesn't hurt."

He slipped his shirt on over his head and Adele helped him with his coat.

"Thank you."

"I'm sorry I didn't hurry back to you last night. I had commitments and things didn't go the way I had planned, but my thoughts were with you." In truth she could barely sleep all night, but it might not be wise to tell him that. "I'm concerned about you and want to help you in any way I can. Would it be at all possible for you to tell me who did this to you? I promise I won't say a word."

As he buttoned his coat, he shrugged, avoiding her eyes. "I

never was a suspicious person and I dislike not trusting people, but when your own family hires someone to—." He broke off and shook his head. When it appeared he wasn't going to continue, Adele sighed.

"Tell me what happened. Please," she whispered.

"Someone tried to kill me. They left me for dead."

"Who?"

"I don't know for sure. I have my suspicions, but I have no proof."

Grai's spirit made a throat-clearing sound, prompting a frown from Grai.

"If I knew for sure, I wouldn't need to hide."

"But why stay here of all places?"

"This is my home. My grandfather left it to me."

"This is yours?" That was not what Auntie Eloise had told her, but her aunt could have been mistaken.

"My Auntie thought it was owned by a Mr. Bonneville. Is that you?"

"Richard Bonneville is my stepfather. And no. He doesn't own it."

Regardless of who owned the estate, one could hardly call these ruins suitable for a home. She looked around, wondering if she had missed seeing a standing structure that he could take shelter in. All she saw was a courtyard of rubble smothered under a thick layer of ice, painted with the browns and blacks of moss and decomposing weeds.

"This is your home? There's nothing here!"

"There's enough."

"You'll freeze to death. Don't you have another place you can go to where you can have a doctor look at your wound?"

He glared at her, a surge of emotion radiated from his eyes. Anger, hurt, despondency?

"If the man who facilitated this attack is who I think he is, he knows where I live and then he'll make certain I die."

Adele picked up her coat, held it on her lap, and studied him. She'd seen criminals before. She'd seen hard men who were selfish and cruel, men who worked in the oyster beds during the day and wasted their bodies on heavy drink at night. Those were the kind of men that murdered or were murdered. Rude, rough, and nasty men. Men with pitted faces and bad breath, with scars from brawls and with hate and rebellion in their eyes.

Grai had none of those traits. He was young, not much older than her, and his skin was smooth, unscathed. He had bright eyes and a quiet reserve, even in his anger. There would be no reason for anyone to murder him.

"Who would want to kill you? I see no reason."

He breathed a laugh and pushed his hair off his face.

"Men who want proprietorship of this estate."

"Then you do own this place?"

He looked at her with an odd sneer. "Is that implausible?"

"No, I was just surprised. My aunt said this property was owned by an incredibly old man who died and now Mr. Bonneville owns it."

"The old man was my grandfather. Cyrus Madison." He took a breath to tell her more, and then looked away. "Who's your aunt?"

"Eloise Barrington. My uncle is Nicholas Barrington. They own the manor on the other side of your fence."

"I know them."

"You do? Then you won't mind coming to stay with us until you can get better."

Grai looked at his spirit, who nodded and smiled as if to tell him yes.

"No," Grai said.

"You'll freeze to death sleeping outside."

"I don't sleep outside." He bowed his head and brushed back his hair.

"Where then?"

"You ask a lot of questions."

"I want to help."

Adele looked past him toward two pillars covered with moss, barely distinguishable from the maple trees. Beyond them, a mound of dirt that resembled a mole's burrow nested into the ground. Some sort of cellar, it seemed to Adele, that had become a living organism like the sprawling roots that twisted around its entrance. This might be his shelter.

"You can help by staying quiet about me being here. Don't tell your aunt, your uncle, nor that kissing cousin of yours. Everyone is a suspect."

Grai's spirit punched him in the arm.

"What?" Grai asked him.

"She's a lady, Grai. She just finished dressing your wound. Show her some respect."

Grai glanced at Adele. "Sorry."

"Oh, think nothing of it," Adele retorted.

"Just please don't tell anyone I'm here. I'm not sure why I made myself known to you. It was probably his fault." He nodded toward the spirit.

Adele tucked her supplies neatly in the bag and snapped it shut. Confused as to whether she should stay and try to find out more, or if she did her part and should go home.

"I brought you some blankets."

Grai nodded. "Thank you."

"Don't you get cold?"

"My body chills, but there's nothing inside of me that cares. He cares. Not I."

Adele studied the person Grai referred to. The translucent image who moved in and around Grai—Grai's likeness, only more colorful, more cheerful, more alive, and friendlier, yet transparent.

She shuddered. The thought of being only half a person with no feelings, and yet having to watch yourself, or someone like yourself experience more of life than you—what a curious predicament.

"Isn't there any way you two could become—you know—one?"

"Why would I want to? I'd rather he left altogether. I would cut that thread that ties him to me with my pocketknife if I could. Go about my life without him. Or die if that's what would happen." Grai turned to her, his hazel eyes vacant, yet something inside of him seemed to cry out for help. "It would be easier, you know if there weren't someone constantly reminding me of my dearth."

"How did your spirit get—broken?"

He stared at her for a long time before he answered, searching her eyes. That emotional-less glower made Adele's spine tingle. Should she even be talking to this person? She liked the spirit who smiled at her from outside of Grai, and how he turned the garden into an oasis in the middle of winter. When he slipped into Grai's body, the man took on his spirit's characteristics. But Grai alone with his morbid, undesirable, and somber glare gave her chills.

He spoke quietly, though, and still maintained a gentleness, even if it were depressing. She had nothing to fear.

"A broken spirit? Now that you put it that way, it makes sense, doesn't it? Has it happened to you? Surely something in your life has broken your spirit?"

"Of course, it has," Adele said without elaborating. "Not quite like you, though."

"Tell me about it."

"Oh—." Adele shook her head and stroked the smooth leather of the medicine bag, avoiding his eyes. If she told him about her parents, he might shun her the way everyone else had.

"Are you ashamed?" His question spurred into the air like a whip lashing across her back. She straightened the pang driving through her body.

Grai's spirit slugged him in the arm again. Grai relented.

"I'm sorry. I didn't mean to return your kindness with my bitterness. It seems no matter what I say anymore it comes out offensive. It's just that I think you should be careful that this doesn't happen to you." Grai gestured toward his spirit, who spun away from him, and had they not been joined together like a man and his shadow the spirit would have fled into the woods. As it were, he went no further than a few feet, stopped, and pivoted around, inching back as Grai continued to explain.

"I think it was more than the attack that severed us. My despondency is just as much a cause and my wound. My spirit wants me to live and I have given up. I don't see a way out of this quandary. I can't go on living with a ghost trailing after me. They'll take my land and sell me to a circus, lock me in a cage for curiosity seekers to gawk over. Or worse, my family will commit me to an asylum. They might, if they're merciful, simply kill me. I assume nothing like this has ever happened to you, that you were never denied an inheritance because a thief pushed their way into your family and stole it? Surely a relative hasn't tried to kill you."

"No, those things haven't happened to me. Quite the opposite, in fact. I spent much of my younger years alone. I certainly don't have an inheritance. None whatsoever, being a woman. Only pittance that my uncle now has power of attorney over, and that he'll use for my room and board when he sells it."

"An injustice," Grai said. "The world is not unbiased. Someday the gentlefolk will live equally alongside men. Slaves won their freedom, someday women will as well. Your parents have died then?"

Adele shrugged knowing that wasn't an answer, but she didn't come here to talk about herself, she came for him.

"Do you really think a relative tried to kill you over an inheritance?" she asked.

"I'm fairly certain the man your aunt claims owns this property hired assailants to do the job. He doesn't like me."

"Your stepfather? That doesn't seem right. Even if this property were worth money, it couldn't be worth a man's life."

"Some people would argue that."

For a moment Grai's spirit joined him. A frown from Grai chased him away. "They're looking for my dead body. Once I die, the deed goes to my mother, who cannot own land, therefore it becomes Richard's. As long as there's no corpse at the morgue, the estate is in probate. Otherwise, my stepfather can sell it."

"Why don't you challenge your stepfather and show him you're alive?"

"Like this? Look at me? I'm near death. It wouldn't take an army to finish me off, and then the rogue would take all that my grandfather worked for. No. I'm staying here incognito. It's the right thing to do until I heal. Until the two of us are one again, or until I die." He nodded toward his spirit, and then as he tucked the end of his scarf into his coat, his gaze rolled over the courtyard, the fountain, the graveyard. "Grandfather made this place an oasis. It wasn't just his house. He took in people who needed a helping hand. Former slaves. People from the tribe who were cheated of their land. He took me in, before the fire. I used to help him with the roses."

Grai's spirit had wandered back to the flower beds. With a hand gentler than any Adele had ever seen in a man he touched one of the dying buds. Slowly the bud opened and like magic unfolded into a sunburst of bright pink and yellow petals. Adele's mouth hung wide, thrilled at the miracle. She looked at Grai, who gazed at his spirit longingly.

"The fool keeps hanging on. Look at him. He thinks the world is a playhouse. Everything he touches turns to gold," Grai laughed slightly, but a sadness crossed his face. "Miracles that no one can see, that need to be hidden. It's real, but it isn't."

When Grai looked at her again, the smile had faded altogether. "If I die, I don't want them to find my body. Let them rot not knowing what happened to me. My mother allowed that man to kill me. It tears me to the core."

"Maybe your mother doesn't know what happened," Adele offered in an attempt to negate such a horrible thought.

He shook his head. "How could she not know?"

"Have you spoken to anyone beside…him…since this happened?" she asked, indicating his spirit.

"No. I've seen no one. Only you."

The distance between them closed. Not that she had moved any nearer to him on the bench, but that he had chosen to tell her secrets that no one else knew, and she more than willingly received him. She made a vow to keep those secrets.

"Your spirit seems to hope for something better." Her words were a breath more than an utterance as she watched another rose come to life.

"Full of optimism. He believes in a world that will let him down. As much as I'd like to be whole again, I don't think his innocence would help me survive. He knows nothing."

"I would think he knows all that you know."

Grai shook his head. "He has no brain, any more than I have feelings, now." Grai's eyes rested on her, a kind of gentleness that you would expect from a grandfather. "I don't like talking about him. Let him do what he wants, leave me to be who I am. If we are ever joined again, things might change."

"Aren't you being somewhat hard on yourself? I mean, it's not your fault someone tried to kill you. And it's not your spirit's fault that he wants to believe in goodness. Maybe we can find out who did attack you. You could be wrong. From what my auntie says, everyone in town is anticipating the railroad coming to Port Summerhill. People are looking for investments, and you own a goodly amount of land. You might have been attacked by someone you never met."

The words of her aunt hovered over her heavy like a storm cloud. She didn't want to tell him that her uncle wanted this property. She didn't want Grai to think that Uncle Nicholas might be as suspicious as anyone else in Port Summerhill. But would her uncle murder someone to get his way? Ever since she found out her parents were killers, trusting people had become difficult. Look at her cousin, Benjamin. He had one objective with her, and she had little to no defense other than to avoid the man. Was her entire family plagued with scandalous intentions?

It could be that Grai's story was a falsehood, too. A stranger hiding out on an abandoned piece of property—with a ghost no less—he could be lying to her. To what end? So that he can stay here and plant heirloom roses, or build a house? It seemed highly unlikely that Grai lied about his situation, and she wondered if spirits could lie?

She regarded the two of them, Grai sitting next to her, his spirit at his side hands folded on his lap. Grai had been studying the pillars that had fallen into the courtyard.

"Those stones will make a good slab for the floor, they just need to be chiseled down some," he said, speaking to his spirit.

"That's a lot of work," his spirit responded.

"A little at a time. I can do it."

"Mustn't open that wound."

Grai nodded.

Adele returned to her thoughts, comforted that she found Grai trustworthy. He'd been a victim of someone in high places—an important person with influence—and had been caught off guard. Wounded, he had no power against the wiles of the wealthy.

"I understand why you don't want to go out in public. It is—I don't know—bizarre to see the two of you severed. But there are ways to avoid having the public see you and still investigate."

"What ways?"

"I could be your legate with the outside world. I could solve this mystery for you."

Grai shook his head and laughed softly.

"I'd be a fool to let a beautiful young lady embark on such a dangerous venture."

"It can't be as dangerous as anything else I've been involved in." She didn't mean to sound so melancholy, but it was true. Living her entire life in a rough sea village, raised by parents who were going to be hanged for murder. Facing a cousin who thought of her as a fallen woman and an uncle who thought of her as his 'property'—the bottom didn't seem to be much lower. What difference did it make if she risked her life? At least if she succeeded she'd have done something worthwhile.

As if the breeze shifted her back into reality, she gasped.

"It's Saturday, isn't it?"

"I suppose? Why? What does that mean?"

She looked wide-eyed into his, the shock that had stunned her in the courtroom a few days ago returned to haunt her. "My parents are being hanged today."

"What?"

Adele shuddered. "At noon." She breathed deeply and held her hand over her mouth. The gallows, the crowd, her parents standing side-by-side, the images crept into her mind. "I didn't want to watch but I'm seeing it in my mind, even now!"

Grai moaned as his spirit rushed into him and he put his arm around her.

"I'm so sorry," he whispered.

"The last time I saw them they were being taken out of the courtroom by men in uniform. I know they committed a crime, but, oh

God!" She saw the noose around their necks and tears leaked from her eyes. She closed them as his arms tightened around her. The tenderness comforted her, and she blinked the vision away. His arm around her soothed her, and she lingered in that space for a moment.

"Thank you," she whispered. "My world has been spinning ever since the trial. I don't know who I am any longer, nor what place I have in life."

"I know the feeling," Grai said, his voice soft and comforting. "And now you must deal with a cousin who treats you ill. What about the rest of your family?"

"My uncle is rough, but he's not altogether rogue. My auntie is kind. It's just my cousin Benjamin who is a cad."

He pulled her closer and rested his chin on her hair, his warm breath tickled her forehead. She felt the tremor of his spirit inside of him.

"The world is a cruel place for the gentlefolk," he whispered. "It's as though if you don't play along with their schemes and hostilities, you get swallowed by them. Somehow we have to rise above it and let them know we're not going to succumb. I'm afraid I haven't yet mastered the craft."

"Nor I," she said.

"No, I think you have."

She pulled away from him, seeing double again as his spirit quivered in and out of him.

"Your trust is innocent and remarkable, both. You went out of your way to help a stranger despite what might happen to you. You even hurt yourself to help me. It's incredible. You don't know who I am? I could be a murderer for all you know."

He said it in such a way that, to Adele, he seemed to be scolding her. Heat rushed to her cheeks. Yes, he could have been a criminal. She knew he was hiding, but she would never have thought him dangerous.

Especially not by the kindness of his spirit. She looked at the phantom who now stood behind Grai. He tilted his head and had a sympathetic pout on his face.

"And I could have been a murderer as well," she argued. "Yet you let me dress your wound. How do you know I didn't rub some sort of poison into you?" She held back a smile until Grai laughed.

"You have me there," he said.

"I choose to trust you, and I'm sympathetic to your cause. I must tell you, while we're on the subject of trust, that my uncle has his eye on this property. He wants to purchase it."

Grai raised his chin and sat upright. The air around them grew suddenly solemn as Grai's spirit sunk into the shadows behind him. "Who does he plan to purchase it from?"

"I don't know any more than what I just told you. The news came from my aunt this morning. They're taking me to a business meeting with bankers from California soon. I might be able to find out there."

Grai rubbed his wound, and worry darkened his face.

"Your uncle doesn't know I'm here does he?"

"No. I didn't even know you were here until yesterday," her voice tapered as he paled. "Oh, please don't think I've come to hurt you. I was only teasing about the poison. And I'm sure my uncle doesn't know anything about you and the situation with your grandfather's estate."

"Adele, I'm feeling ill and I think you should leave." He stood and picked up the blankets Adele had given him.

"Thank you for these blankets." He waited for his spirit who remained in the wisteria arbor creating tiny lavender buds under the frost. When his spirit didn't respond to him, he walked away and seemed to vanish in the dense undergrowth near the graveyard.

Adele remained on the bench, the medicine bag on her lap, her shoulders slumped, staring vacuously at his receding figure. "What did I do wrong?" she asked.

"Oh, don't worry about him, he needs to mull over his problems and that will put him to sleep soon. He needs his rest," Grai's spirit said, though he didn't direct his statement to her, but talked to the wisteria blossoms he created. "His troubles will vanish temporarily, but you and I can spend time together, getting to know each other. We'll be in his dreams."

He looked at her, his silly transparent body, his bouncy curls, and his smile.

"He'll like that. He likes dreaming about lovely things and he thinks you're lovely."

She gave the spirit her attention and he coaxed a smile from her. If anyone knew Grai, it would be his spirit, wouldn't it?

Frolic

Imagine blushing because of something an apparition said. Adele's cheeks flamed, and she couldn't help but smile. Grai's spirit tugged on a wisteria vine and shook it until a long dangly shoot sprung out and blossomed into a multitude of delicate flowers sending a delicious fragrance into the air.

"This wisteria has been here for at least fifty years," he explained. "One of the many prized endeavors of our grandfather, as is most of the vegetation you see here. A more talented horticulturist you wouldn't find. Port Summerhill should have commended him, given him a trophy for having the most prolific garden. Many a home in this town had cuttings and seeds that Grandfather Madison propagated from his heirloom plants. They flourish to this day in gardens everywhere. The people of this town owe the allure of Port Summerhill to him."

"He must have been a delightful man."

"He was the best grandfather anyone could hope to have. I think the love that he showed for nature was an indication of his gentle soul."

"I wish I could have known him," Adele said.

"He would have loved you."

He released the stalk and let it bounce overhead and dangle from the arbor.

"Come," he said and guided her to the fountain.

"I hope you understand Grai's passion for the estate, and for his grandfather. It's part of who he is. He spent the last few years studying architecture so that he could rebuild these ruins to what they once were. He's near identical to the old man in talent and devotion." The spirit's voice faded as he stared at the fountain lost in thought.

"Tell me more about Grai," Adele pleaded, hoping to coax him out of his gloominess.

Grai's spirit raised an eyebrow and grinned.

"He'll be thrilled that you asked!" he said. "And probably livid that I answered but I've dealt with his temper before. There's no need to tell you more about him. I can show you, instead, Come with me."

Adele followed the specter as he floated toward the woods and disappeared into the snow-laden forest. Once enough light peeked through the trees from above, he became visible again. The wintry landscape behind him painted outlandish patterns on his face. He wore the same clothes Grai did, minus the color of the waistcoat, for nothing opaque adhered to him. There appeared to be no wound, though, no visible sign of having been hurt, which seemed curious to Adele. He traveled quickly and Adele had difficulty keeping pace with him for he could penetrate right through the trees, snowbanks, and any other obstacle in his way. Adele had to leap over the underbrush to catch him. When they approached the edge of the woods where the forest floor met the grassy hills of the graveyard, she caught her breath and sighed. She could have taken the trail!

"This is Grai's family," his spirit said sweeping his hand toward the tombstones. Not more than thirty monuments dotted the field, though there could be more under the ice and snow. Each of the gravestones swelled out of the mulch a different shape, some merely a rock with a name carved or a plate held into place by plugs. Most were sculpted from marble or a simple granite slab. Three wooden crosses jutted out of the snow among them.

"The largest cross mark's his father's grave. You can't see it from here, and it's a bit muddy to walk up to it, so I won't take you any further, but the pattern and design is delicately carved. Not a year goes by that Grai doesn't make another memorial for him. Grai was thirteen when his father died."

"And Richard Bonneville became his stepdad when?"

"Oh, just a year ago. His mother raised Grai by herself. It was just the two of them—of us— for so many years, which is why he feels she forsook him. You see, Grai worked in the oyster beds when he was a youngster to provide for our little family and later he worked to see himself through an apprenticeship with a noted architect in Tacoma. He made a good living and gained respect of our neighbors. When our grandfather fell ill with consumption, Grai spent as much time as he could with him. Mother could have waited to marry again. She knew there'd be an inheritance for Grai. Once she wed Bonneville, things got complicated. The man had been so controlling that mother went daft and began holding seances and talking to ghosts." He chuckled a bit and then forced himself to stop. "Not ghosts like me. I'm a living spirit. She talks to dead ones, the kind of ghosts who drive people out of windows three stories high or who pit themselves into blazing fires. Demons I like to think of them."

"Are there such phantoms that do that?"

Grai's spirit shrugged. "I don't know. Grai and I decided not to entertain them if there are. In any case, Grandfather hated Richard for the way he treated his daughter and refused to leave this estate to him. Grai just recently found the Will validating grandfather's requests."

"And Grai, of course, is the beneficiary?"

"The entire domain, and a few other items, were left to us, yes. It would make perfect sense for Bonneville to have Grai murdered. The inheritance would return to Grai's mother and since women cannot own property, he would have full power over all of this."

"And so, without a body to prove he's dead, the estate hangs in limbo?" Adele surmised.

"Exactly. For now, anyway. After a certain amount of time, depending on how much the lawyer is paid, if no corpse is found, probate would commence, or Richard could request a hearing and get things moving quicker, which is what Grai thinks he'll do. Grai fears as soon as he shows his face, whoever tried to kill him would finish the job."

"How incredibly sad. But how long can he go on like this? How long can the both of you go on like this?"

"I will go on forever. It's Grai's body we need to worry about. We're too young to die. I suppose our stubbornness is keeping us in a state of indecision."

"I would call it tenacity. A will to live is not anything to shun."

Grai's spirit smiled. "I like the way you think. You're not only lovely, but you're also intelligent. I hope to influence Grai concerning you. I think the three of us could be particularly good friends."

She blushed again as his eyes looked deep into hers. The connection gave her chills, and so she changed the subject.

"When did the manor burn to the ground?" Adele asked.

"Just before they took grandfather to the sanitorium five years ago where he recently died of tuberculosis. These ruins all happened because of an earthquake which toppled some of the structures and also started the fire."

"When did his…your…grandfather die?"

"A month ago."

"With feeling betrayed by his mother, and at odds with her new husband, his grandfather's death must have been traumatic for Grai."

"Yes, just as your parent's death is for you. I am sorry." Grai's spirit spoke quietly.

My parent's death…the words stung, and she gasped. "Good Lord!" She bit her lip, realizing that the sun was directly overhead. Noon!

"It's happened, hasn't it? Just now! They're dead!" The trial and knowing that they were going to die had traumatized her, and she had little hope that they'd survive. But the fact that this very moment, not far from here, the sentence was being carried out. The awareness jolted her, and then rushed through her like a tidal wave. She covered her face with trembling hands, her heart cut in two. She sank to the ground and hunched over in the snow. Icy crystals adhered to her clothes and the dam that had swelled inside of her burst with tears uncontrollable.

"Oh dear, what did I do," Grai's spirit groaned as he swirled around her. "I'm so sorry! I didn't mean to hurt you."

She didn't hear him, completely unaware of her surroundings, she mourned and remained in that state for a long while. The shadows grew longer as the sun fell lower and the cold crept through her coat and stockings. She shivered without realizing why.

Memories of her childhood played havoc with her mind—taking her back to the days when she sat on her father's lap by the hearth listening to fairy tales. Or when she'd wash clothes in a tub outside with her mother dragging the dripping garments to a rope that hung between the eaves of their house and the maple tree. She remembered days sitting on the hillside overlooking the sea, waiting for her parents to come home. On those days she had to do all the sweeping and dusting and firewood gathering by herself. In the winter she would start the fire, as hard as it was, with damp wood and coals they kept in a cast-iron kettle. She'd spend long hours reading by lantern light or pacing on the porch waiting for her mother or father to appear from wherever it was they went. They told her they were working yet how could they have and been so poor? She remembered the day not so long ago when her mother and father came home with blood on their hands and how they told her they helped the neighbor butcher a lamb, but they didn't bring home any meat that evening, and she wondered how selfish the neighbor was for not sharing.

She should have suspected something, but she didn't. They were her parents. They housed her and clothed her and there was always food on the table even if only shellfish and berries they had foraged from the forests. Her parents, even in her teens, were all she knew of life.

She wiped her eyes as these last images quieted her tears. Her head ached from crying and eventually she looked up to see a darkened sky and tiny snowflakes floating in the air. Grai's spirit had taken residence in the branches of a fir tree near her.

"You waited?" she asked. "All my sobbing and you remained by my side?"

"How could I leave you?" He floated from the tree and sat in the snow next to her. "You needed me, if for nothing else but to be by your side."

"That's kind of you. I must look like a wailing banshee."

"Not so."

"It's seeing these tombstones and talking about death…," she said.

"See, it *is* my fault."

"No. I had to cry. I had to get it out of my system. It was good for me to be here. Uncle Nicholas didn't want me to cry over them."

"Why?"

"He says it's a dishonor to the man he murdered and to the town who condemned them. I can understand, it's just…hard."

"Do you want to talk about it more?" he asked. "I don't mind. Share the burden with me. It won't be too hard for a spirit." He laughed and flexed his transparent muscles. "It might even help you."

She shrugged. What harm could come from talking to a phantom about her parents? Grai told her everything about himself without reluctance. She could do the same. It might be healing.

"I suppose," she answered.

"So, tell me this. Were your parents accused falsely?"

"No. They really did murder someone in cold blood."

The spirit darkened when he frowned. "Who? Why?"

"I don't know why. I never had a chance to talk to either of them. They told me they had been at the neighbor's butchering a lamb that day. To explain the blood," she shivered and wiped her eyes. If only that simple gesture could erase the bloody scene out of her mind.

"Oh dear," Grai's spirit whispered. "It must have been horrible for you."

"Now it is. I didn't think so at the time because I believed their lie."

"Who was this unfortunate victim?"

"An old man who lived on the edge of town. Professor Reinhardt was his name."

Grai's spirit jerked back in surprise, and all sorts of colors flickered through him like sparks of fire. "Professor Reinhardt from Port Galleon?"

"You know him?"

"Oh, my dear Adele. Professor Reinhardt was our grandfather's business partner."

Adele gaped at him. "No!"

"Yes. The two traded in gold together. He was a genuinely nice man. Grai met him a few times. Oh, he will be devastated to hear this. And that your family had a hand in his death. Not a good thing for us."

"I had nothing to do with it, I swear."

"Yes, I believe you. You would have no reason to be involved in such a crime. Were your parents alone in this murder?"

"There was one other. A man named Delaney. He got away."

"Oh, this is bad. Unbelievably bad."

"Do you know him?"

"I've heard the name. Grandfather mentioned him occasionally. I think he was the professor's intern. Delaney would know about the estate. He would have heard about Grai. Maybe even about the Will."

"Do you think maybe he's the one who attacked Grai?"

"Mm, could be, could be. Our list of enemies grows." The spirit's eyes began to rove over the terrain, suspicious and frightened. "No one followed you, did they? No one knows you came here, do they?"

"No, I don't think so."

"Well, there's nothing we can do about this now except hope that Grai doesn't wake up until you leave. I will have to break the news to him gently. It would be better if you weren't here when I do."

"You think he'll be suspicious of me because of it?" Adele rose out of the snow and brushed off her skirt.

"I don't know. I hope not, but there are so many complications now. So many. Come back to the garden with me," he said. "Come. Let's get away from the graveyard for your sake. Mourning has its place, but we shouldn't be downtrodden by so much death. Come!"

Adele pulled a hankie from her coat pocket to wipe her eyes and blow her nose, and then she walked with him. Grai's spirit didn't float ahead of her this time but stayed by her side so closely that the fervor of his energy lifted her spirits.

"I am sorry about your parents. This is a day of calamity for you, and I hope you look for healing. You must understand that death is a part of life. When you see it from my perspective, it isn't all that bad."

"You're not dead," Adele reminded him.

"I'm not going to die," he said. "I'll just move on when it's time, and Grai won't even know what happened. Instead of me being part of him, he'll be a part of me." He had a sincere grin and winked at her when she looked at him. "See, then I'll be calling the moves and he'll have to submit to me."

She laughed and his smile grew wider. "There you go. There's a smile."

He flew onward now that they were at the fountain, and touched not just the roses this time, but the ground where crocuses sprung up from under frozen maple leaves and popped open, daffodil blades pierced through the soil and exposed their yellow blossoms, and he even woke a dozen bluebirds who took to flight over her head. As a finishing touch, he reached out to her. A warm breeze tickled her fingers leaving a bouquet of dahlias, lilacs, and forget-me-nots in her hands.

"For you, my sweet," he said gently. "May they bring restoration to your heart. I must visit Grai. Don't worry. I will convince him you're our friend."

"Please convince him I want to help him. I want to find whoever attempted to murder him and make sure they will never hurt him again. I hate that anyone would be so cruel."

"I'll tell him."

Adele breathed in the fragrance of her bouquet and joined eyes with the spirit. "You are Grai, aren't you?" she asked.

"His very essence, even though he denies my influence all too often. He won't ever escape me."

"I hope your differences can be resolved soon. You...he...is a wonderful person."

"He is. We will," the spirit said. "If not in this life, the next."

"Don't! Please. Don't talk about dying. I would very much like to spend time with Grai here and now. I'm becoming fond of him and enjoying your company."

The spirit's smile faded, and his eyes grew more intense, brighter as if they were leaving the spirit form and becoming real. "That will warm his heart, Adele. Thank you. He needs something, or someone to live for."

No sooner had he said that then she heard a rustling in the bushes near the gate. When she looked over her shoulder, a snowball hit the ground in front of her—giggling followed, and then the sound of footsteps— children running away.

A wave of fear crossed over her and when she looked back,

Grai's spirit had vanished, but the bouquet remained in her hands. She picked up the medicine bag from the bench and raced for the gate, nearly slipping on the ice. When she could see her uncle's yard, Peter and Maggie were sprinting across the patio headed for the house.

What had they seen and what would they say?

Peter

Adele stomped the snow off her boots on the storm porch and caught her breath before she entered the kitchen. With Peter and Maggie visiting their grandparents, it meant the entire family had gathered. Uncle Nicholas might be home as well. Her heart beat hard, worried that the children had seen her talking to Grai's spirit and would tell, terrified of what the family's reaction would be.

What troubled her more was that Grai might admonish her because her parents murdered Professor Reinhardt, his grandfather's good friend. Grai may choose to never see her again! That would hurt more than any punishment Uncle Nicholas could administer. It seemed the entire world would soon compress her into a dried-out sponge. She'd be a friend to no one, and useless to all.

She shut the kitchen door quietly and hid the medicine bag under a cupboard, intending to return it to its rightful place when she was alone. Mei Ling greeted her with a quick nod while stirring onions in a cast-iron skillet.

"Smells delicious," Adele said as she opened cupboards looking for a vase. She found an old stein instead, and so poured water from the pitcher and arranged the flowers in it.

"Fresh flowers?" Mei Ling ceased stirring and stared at the bouquet.

Adele smiled.

"In winter?"

"You never know what you'll find under the hoarfrost."

Mei Ling shook her head and resumed cooking.

"Lots of strange things happen here," she mumbled.

"Like flowers in winter?"

She nodded. "Flowers in winter are odd but good. Some things not so good."

Adele paused and watched the woman toss the vegetables, her arms moving in rhythm, one mixing the food, the other rotating the pan.

"Tell me more."

Mei Ling pouted and glimpsed at Adele. "What do you want to know?"

"What other odd things are you referring to? Did you see something?"

"Lights sometimes."

"Where?" Had Mei Ling seen Grai's spirit's lights?

"Next door. That's not all. Lots more things. Haunted things."

"Like what?"

Mei Ling grunted, focusing on the food she cooked. The more she talked, the faster she stirred. "Screams in the night. Cups turn upside down when no one moves them. Dead people walking through walls."

"You saw all of this?"

She nodded.

"And it happens where?"

"Everywhere. In the bunkhouse, your uncle's hotel. Everywhere. The entire town whispers about it."

"All of Port Summerhill?"

"Maybe."

"Do my aunt and uncle know?"

She shrugged. "They don't believe."

Adele hadn't heard that ghosts plagued the entire town, but then she spent no time with residents of Port Summerhill, although Grai said his mother holds seances.

"You asked your uncle to learn to cook with me?" Mei Ling asked as she dropped pieces of meat into the pan and wiped her hands on her apron.

"Not yet. Soon!"

"Good! Holidays come too soon. I need help."

"Splendid!" After she solved the mystery behind Grai she'd hide away in the kitchen for the rest of her life and avoid Benjamin and Uncle Nicholas both. She picked up the vase to carry into the dining hall, but Mei Ling made a high-pitched sound, startling her.

"Leave flowers in the kitchen."

"Why?"

"Good luck," she said.

Adele laughed and set the vase on the counter.

"Bad luck if your aunt and uncle see them." She shook her head and clicked her tongue.

"Oh!" No doubt a bouquet of winter flowers would cause confusion.

There would be no good luck for Adele today for as soon as she stepped into the living room, Benjamin caught her off guard. Dressed in a blue silk waistcoat, his white shirt buttoned tight and a bow tie adorning his neck, her cousin stood warming himself by the fireplace. His eyes widened when he saw her, and his lips bent into a crooked smile.

Where had everyone else disappeared to?

Tossing his golden hair back with a shake of his head, he greeted her. "Adele!"

He took a step toward her.

"Don't touch me," Adele warned as he approached. She stood her ground. *A cougar chases a doe only when she runs,* her father once told her.

Before Benjamin got too near, he stopped and look down the hall and Adele followed his gaze. Shadows and voices in a room off the corridor indicated the family had gathered in the parlor. Benjamin wouldn't dare try anything in the house, would he?

"I hear you're going to the soiree with us tomorrow evening," he said as he drew her attention away from the activity down the hall.

"You're going?" Adele asked, none too pleased.

"Of course."

"I might become suddenly ill that day. What time is this event so I can plan my malady?"

"Nonsense."

"I don't care to be in the same room with you. Ever." She headed for the parlor, impeded by his arm around her waist.

"Let go of me," she hissed.

He pulled her close and whispered in her ear. "The family plans to marry you off to one of the elite's sons. I can make sure you get in the wealthiest arms if you do me a favor."

"The only favor I might do you is by filling your boots with petrified cow dung and having the mules haul you to the river. Get your hands off of me." She tried pushing his arm away, but he resisted.

She raised her brow. "Did you forget I come from the pit of the earth?" she breathed. "I still have friends lurking in the shadows of Port Galleon waiting to attack rogues like you."

He let her go. But that might have been because Aunt Eloise called him.

"What's going on in here?" her aunt asked just as Benjamin stepped away from Adele.

"Nothing. I was simply asking Adele if she knew about the stolen necklace."

"What necklace?" Adele asked.

106

"We don't know that anyone stole it, Benjamin. Lila may have simply misplaced it," Aunt Eloise gave the two of them a dubious frown. "Adele, please come with me. Your dress is just about done, but I need you to try it on."

Adele glanced in the parlor as she passed by, her heart skipping a beat when she saw Lila and the children conferring with Uncle Nicholas. If the children were relaying what they saw earlier, Adele might face another chastisement. She hurried, hoping none of the family saw her, although Benjamin slid into the room after she passed by.

Aunt Eloise led her into a guest room further down the hall and shut the door. Her aunt spread out the gown of silk on the bed, and Adele gasped when she saw it.

"Oh, Aunt Eloise, is that for me to wear?"

"It's yours to keep. I would hope you would wear it. I'm not doing this for my health. Here, undress and come stand on the stool. Your corset is on the chair."

"I have one on already," Adele argued.

"Trust me. You'll need this one with that bodice." Aunt Eloise handed her the corset to put on. An unusual shape, it matched the princess bodice on the dress with boning that extended off the waistline to the hips.

"As if things couldn't get any worse," Adele moaned as she hurriedly undressed out of her woolens.

Aunt Eloise fitted the evening bodice over the slim-lined corset, and Adele, shocked at the exposure, held her hand over her chest. "Auntie, I'm not used to this. Must it be so revealing?"

"This dress reveals extraordinarily little, it only suggests. We can't have you tucked away in clothing that's not even fit for a maid." Aunt Eloise tightened the laces as Adele held her breath. "Not only is this get-together a celebration for the railroad, an invitational for politicians, bankers, and leaders of our community, but it is also your debut." She leaned close to Adele and whispered in her ear. "You cannot expect a man to be interested in you if he sees you have nothing of interest. Trust me, Adele."

Not sure she wanted a man interested in anything a dress might 'suggest', Adele tensed while her aunt tightened the corset and slipped on the bodice which had its share of lace, buttons, and tiny pearls woven through an off-white braid. The gathered lace covered much of her neckline, and so she didn't feel as exposed as she thought she'd be.

The skirt itself hung in layered drapery, alternating between soft minty silk and a lusher satin, wrapping around in back with only the hint of bustle and a small train. When Aunt Eloise held the mirror up for her to see, the only thing that looked out of place was her matted hair and eyes that divulged the waterfall of tears she had shed that afternoon. The rest of her image challenged the beauty of any aristocrat young woman of her day.

"It's so pretty!" she exclaimed.

"My skills are improving with each dress I make. I'm glad you like it." She took a wooden box of pins from out of her sewing basket while Adele inspected the fabric, the lace, and the tiny pearl buttons on the sleeves. "Now hold still and tell me what's going on."

Aunt Eloise's voice lost its friendliness.

"What do you mean?"

"You and Benjamin are becoming much too intimate."

"I can't stand him, Auntie. He pushes himself on me and then he threatens me."

Aunt Eloise stepped back and looked Adele in the eye. With pins held between her lips, her auntie's frown sent a chill up Adele's spine.

She let the pins fall into her hand.

"How long has this been going on?"

"The very first day I arrived he accused me of being a woman of the night and that he…" she choked on her words. "He wanted to…"

"That's a dire accusation, Adele." Aunt Eloise was kind enough to interrupt so that Adele needn't go into detail.

"I wouldn't accuse him of such a thing if it weren't true."

"And why didn't you come to me?"

"I'm afraid of him, Auntie. He's extraordinarily strong."

"I'll discuss this with Nicholas."

"No! Please!" That would be the last thing she needed as she feared her uncle as much as she feared her cousin. If her uncle thought she was lying, he would defend his son and would punish her. Worse, Benjamin would seek revenge.

"I'll find the right time and place, preferably after this social. But we need to address these matters if they're true. And if they're not," she looked Adele in the eye. "Well, if not, then we need to address that as well."

"Uncle Nicholas won't believe me," Adele whispered.

"You don't know what he'll believe."

No, but she could guess. It's a man's world. She held her tongue though and watched her aunt pin the hem. Torn between wanting her cousin to stop propositioning her, and avoiding another confrontation with her uncle, she fretted, though the dilemma was now out of her hands.

"Father wants to talk with you, Adele." Benjamin's overly radiant smile caused a growl in her stomach when he peeked into the room. Aunt Eloise didn't seem too pleased to have him interrupt, either.

"She'll be there when I'm finished, Benjamin."

"Father's not a patient man," he told his mother and was met with the eyes of a dragon. "Just letting you know."

"I know your father better than you do. Leave us in peace or this will take twice as long," Aunt Eloise scolded. Benjamin dodged out of the room.

"He's becoming more and more mulish the older he gets. I'm not sure where he gets it from, but I'm tired of it."

"He seems to enjoy the suffering of others," Adele mumbled.

"He's his father's son." Aunt Eloise agreed.

After pushing the last pin through the hem and measuring around the bottom of the dress once more, she stepped back.

"It will be a fitting garb for you, Adele. I'm hoping you will catch the eye of one of the Travis boys. Fine gentlemen they are and are in line for enough wealth to keep you satisfied."

"I'm not after wealth, Auntie."

"You say that now, but you've been poor all your life and you suffer the trauma of your parent's crimes. I think the best thing that can happen to you is for you to marry someone who can afford you a suitable home and enough money to maintain it." She touched Adele's cheek tenderly. "You have much to offer a man, but you need a gentle one. Know that I'm looking out for your best interest."

"Yes, ma'am. But...."

"But what?"

"This dress, and going out in public, I'm not sure it's right."

"What are you talking about?"

"Today my parents died. Shouldn't I be wearing black for a while? In mourning."

Aunt Eloise sighed and took her hand. "Those traditions don't apply here in these western territories. They are old-fashioned and inhibiting, especially for a young lady as yourself."

"Uncle Nicholas doesn't want me to mourn for my parents, does he?"

She sighed heavily and took a moment to respond. "I have to admit, mourning for your parents would be awkward here in Port Summerhill. The execution was public, Adele. Everyone in town knows who they were and what they did, and some residents knew Professor Reinhardt. The dignities your uncle associates with were outraged when they found out what happened. Better not to remind them of your relationship which is what you in black would do. You'd be making a mockery of the professor, throwing guilt upon the judge, condemning the executioners, and embarrassing the town. Your parents were the guilty ones, not the rest of the world for carrying out the sentence."

Aunt Eloise slipped the dress over her head carefully and laid it on the bed.

"Turn around," she said, and untied the corset.

"You can't even mourn your sister."

"We weren't close. Now hurry, change your clothes, and answer your uncle's summons. We have company coming this evening."

"Who?"

"One of your uncle's business partners. Richard Bonneville and his wife Lucille. We need to make a good impression."

Stunned, Adele stared at her aunt as she spread the gown carefully on the bed. Grai's parents were coming here? The people whom Grai thinks paid to have him murdered? Adele closed her mouth. She mustn't look so surprised.

Her aunt left the room without another word, and Adele changed back into her woollies, which had taken on the smell of sheep in a thunderstorm. She shouldn't have rolled about in the snow that afternoon wailing like a ghoul, especially since she had so few dresses and no others that were dry. She would see what her uncle wanted and then change into something more appropriate for the evening.

When Adele stepped into the parlor, Uncle Nicholas had his back to her, and Lila sat on the davenport with an arm around Maggie while Butterscotch curled up on the young one's lap. Peter stood beside his grandfather and folded his arms when she walked in. He too wore a bow tie and held his chin up just like his uncle Benjamin had earlier. She gave him a special grimace.

Please don't let this meeting be about Grai's ghost!

"Adele, have you seen a pearl necklace with a cameo?" Lila asked.

"No."

"Well, Peter seems to think he saw you with a necklace just like mine this morning out in the garden, and I'd like to know why."

"I have no idea why Peter thinks what he does," Adele said, her full focus on the boy. "But I've never seen your necklace, and I have no need for such an item. I don't wear jewelry."

Lila sprung off the couch, stepped in front of Adele, and folded her arms.

"It's a valuable jewel, Adele. Don't toy with me."

Adele met Lila's piercing blue eyes and widened hers.

"I don't steal, and if I did, I wouldn't steal anything of yours. I like you, Lila. I would hope we could be friends. I wanted to thank you for choosing the fabric of my dress and trying on the bodice. I—,"

"I want my necklace back! It had more sentimental value than anything else."

Lila had such a pale complexion it took little for her cheeks to flame.

"I would be glad to help you look for it."

"She knows where it is, mother," Peter mumbled.

"Hush, Peter," Uncle Nicholas spoke for the first time. "This is between the women."

"I saw her with it, Grandpa. She's a liar."

"You must have been mistaken, Peter," Adele said calmly. The room had gotten stuffy and hot. She felt perspiration trickle down her side under her dress.

Uncle Nicholas took the boy's hand and walked to the door. "Come, Maggie." He gave Adele a strange look before he left. The three walked out of the room, but not without an over-the-shoulder sneer from Peter. Adele wanted to pick the boy up and throw him through the window. What ill did he have toward her to cause so much trouble?

"If it doesn't turn up by tomorrow, I'm going to search your room," Lila said.

"Search it now," Adele challenged her.

"No. I'll give you the opportunity to make it re-appear."

Adele shook her head and sneered. "I don't have it."

"Look, cousin, my mother and father have bent over backward to give you another start in life. They've provided much more than you deserve, it seems. Such audacity to take advantage of their goodness. That's on them, though. They are more forgiving than I am. You're up against a firing squad with me. I'm friends with the marshal in Port Summerhill. If I find that you've pilfered my necklace, I'll file charges against you. You can wade about in the same swamp your parents came from. I'll not have you tainting my family. If it were up to me, you wouldn't be here."

She stormed out of the room, her pretty blond curls bouncing over her shoulders to the rhythm of rage, leaving Adele about to retch again.

Adele could find the necklace if she scavenged through the house, but then Lila would accuse her of theft. At the moment, she wanted to hide in the tower, but to do that, she'd have to walk through the living room to get to the stairs, the entire family might be waiting to pounce on her.

Adele waited a moment to collect herself. Lila's words cut deep. How could her family have garnered so much hostility toward her in such a short amount of time? What did she do?

Fortunately, only Maggie was in the living room playing with the cat by the fire, and Peter sat smugly on the couch playing with a pocket watch. It might help if she could make peace with the boy. She pushed all of her anxiety to the bottom of her stomach and approached Peter with a gentle smile.

"Peter, why did you lie to your mother?"

He didn't answer.

"Why don't you like me, Peter?"

The boy pulled his attention away from his toy and looked at her. "No one likes you. You're from Port Galleon, where murderers live. You shouldn't be here."

That hurt! But he's just a child responding with an attitude he's learned from others. She could ignore that, tolerate it. What she had a hard time doing was living with the consequences of such attitudes. "Peter, I've done nothing to you."

"You're mean to my Uncle Benjamin."

How could she explain to a little boy why she scuffled with his favorite uncle? She watched him snap open the watch, push the hands around in a circle, and close it again.

"Where did you get that?"

"Not telling," he said.

When he flipped closed the lid, Adele leaned in closer.

"That's not a toy," she whispered, regarding the item which seemed way too valuable for a boy Peter's age to be playing with. The inscription on the cover—CM—was someone's initials, and a glimmering red stone, a ruby, adorned the plate. Adele wasn't an expert in metals, but it appeared to be made of gold.

"Tell me how you got that watch, Peter. It's beautiful. Did someone give it to you?"

"I found it."

"Where?"

He snickered and stuck the watch in his pocket, jumped off the couch, and left the room at a run, no doubt to find his mother.

Soon after, Lila and Garth took the children home. Mei Ling

busied herself in the kitchen preparing snacks for the evening's company, and Adele went to the tower to find something to wear that didn't smell.

The Mirror

A unt Eloise paced in front of the hearth while Uncle Nicholas sat in the rocker reading the Daily Herald. Adele sat on the davenport, not sure what to think. Judging by her aunt's unrest, the evening might not end well. It might not even begin well!

"Settle down, Eloise. It's only the Bonneville's," Uncle Nicholas grumbled. He didn't lower the newspaper when he spoke, but he peeked around it with a grimace aimed at his wife.

"I wish you hadn't invited the both of them. You know how Lucille is."

"I'm confident she'll be respectful. If not, Richard can set her in her place."

"Richard is oblivious."

"Abusive," is what Grai's spirit had revealed. The night should be extremely interesting.

Adele observed her aunt with curiosity. She hadn't seen her so apprehensive over meeting someone before. Up to this point, Aunt Eloise had displayed calm and graciousness even when confronting Uncle Nicholas in his rage and Adele considered her a role model. To see her aunt this distressed was bothersome.

Mrs. Bonneville would soon walk into their home, and the

man whom Grai believes hired a ruffian to kill him would be with her. Adele had her own misgivings about the woman who betrayed Grai. She couldn't help but take his defense. If the Bonnevilles didn't hire someone to kill him, they certainly made his life miserable.

As she watched her aunt pace back and forth in front of the hearth, Adele vowed she would control her temper, and her tongue.

The sound of horses outside drowned her thoughts, and soon a bold knock at the door sent Mei Ling scurrying to the foyer.

"The roads are slick tonight, my friend," a voice called out when the door opened, and a gust of cold air swept inside. Uncle Nicholas rose, and Aunt Eloise gestured for Adele to stand.

"Your ride was a safe one, I surmise?" her uncle responded.

"As safe as any ice skater on a frozen lake would expect." The men laughed.

Aunt Eloise wrung her hands.

Richard Bonneville strolled into the living room with an air of confidence. A short man with bright red hair and a mustache that curled up to his nostrils. He tossed his hat on the coat rack and shook hands with Uncle Nicholas. Adele visualized him slipping a bag of coins to a group of evil mercenaries while laughing and offering a friendly handshake. Her lips curled into a snarl.

The two men slapped each other's arms in greeting and then Richard helped his wife with her coat, hung it on the rack, and removed his own.

"Eloise, it's so good to see you again,"

Mrs. Bonneville entered the living room and moved toward the hearth. A very tall woman who flaunted a luxurious black crepe dress and wore a small black hat with a black veil which she swept away from her face. Around her neck were jet beads and a gold locket hung from them at her collarbone. She wore a musty perfume that, to Adele, attempted to conceal the stench of the abuses she afflicted on her son.

"Lucille, I'm pleased you decided to come and visit." Aunt Eloise offered her a smile which came across sincere. Aunt Eloise could never hide her civility, even if she wanted to.

"And this must be your niece. What is her name?"

"Yes, Adele, this is Mrs. Bonneville."

Adele curtsied but said nothing. She wasn't so sure she was pleased to meet the woman, so why lie?

"Adele?" Lucille approached her. A fair-skinned woman with loose, sandy curls like Grai's which she pulled back into a mountain for her hat to sit upon. She had a pointed nose and brown beady eyes, not handsome like her son's hazel eyes. Grai must have gotten his good looks from his father.

"Richard and I attended your parent's execution. You poor child. I'm surprised that you've already withdrawn from your liability of mourning? Or have you not yet begun?" She muttered, but she might as well have shouted for all the pain she caused.

Adele, stupefied, had no response. What could she say? This was Uncle Nicholas' guest, and if she hit the woman in the mouth, there would be consequences.

"Adele is still settling in, Lucille," Aunt Eloise explained.

"If you'll excuse us, ladies, Richard and I will be in the parlor discussing business." Uncle Nicholas gave Aunt Eloise a raised brow, an imperious look at Mrs. Bonneville, and placed hors d'oeuvres on his plate. He then led Richard away. Bonneville's teacup clattered as he followed Uncle Nicholas. It seemed the two men couldn't wait to be in the privacy of their own company. Adele would rather go with them. She could learn if they were scheming any more ill will toward Grai if they'd let her sit in the parlor with them, but it wasn't for her to ask. No, her station was with this strange woman in black who had given birth to Grai.

"Settling in? Who else is settling in, Eloise?"

"What do you mean?"

Lucille gestured toward the mirror. "You should know."

Aunt Eloise rolled her eyes and guided Lucille to the table.

"What about our mirror?" Adele asked under her breath.

"Adele, hush," Aunt Eloise whispered, "I'll explain later. Please, Lucille! Care for a tea cake? We can sit on the couch and discuss our plans for the party."

Aunt Eloise poured Lucille a cup of tea and the two sat down on the davenport. Adele sat across from them on the rocking chair, thankful that Butterscotch jumped on her lap and gave her a distraction.

"I came here with Richard tonight for a specific purpose, Eloise," Lucille began. She barely tasted her tea, pinkie out, before setting the cup down. "I won't be attending the festivities, nor will I be able to assist you with planning."

"I'm sorry to hear that. Is it because of your son?"

"Indeed, it is. I am overwhelmed with grief over his death."

Aunt Eloise lost her formality at that moment, and she sighed heavily. "I'm so sorry, Lucille. I didn't know that they had confirmed his passing."

"There's no sign of him anywhere. He wouldn't just disappear, and the items found at the crime scene were a sure indicator that someone murdered him. I'm beside myself, as you can see."

Lucille stroked the locket around her neck and broke down in tears. "He was such a good boy. I'm afraid I treated him unfairly."

Adele shuffled in her chair, biting her tongue, and wishing her aunt would give her a chore to tend to so she could excuse herself.

"Are there suspects?" Aunt Eloise asked.

"The marshal says they can't investigate without a body. Oh—" She moaned. "My dear sweet son." She nearly spilled the contents of her cup, and so Aunt Eloise took it from her and set it on the end table.

Aunt Eloise glanced at Adele, a look of exasperation on her face, and moved closer to the woman, putting her arm around her as Lucille sobbed into her hankie.

"Adele, please bring a damp facecloth for this poor woman," she said.

Adele rose and hurried to the water basin in the kitchen, found a facecloth, poured water on it, and brought it to the weeping woman. Lucille took a moment from her wailing to regard Adele.

"I don't understand why you two are so cold-hearted," she said.

"Cold-hearted?" Aunt Eloise asked.

"Well, look at her, Eloise! Why this child refuses to give respect to her departed parents is beyond me," Lucille moaned. "And you, Eloise. That was your sister! Oh, how will you ever survive this atrocity!"

"Wipe her face, Adele," Aunt Eloise instructed, the gentleness gone from her tone.

Adele knelt in front of Lucille and lifted the veil that had fallen during her lament. She dabbed the woman's cheeks and eyes softly with the cloth. The woman snatched the linen from her. When Adele backed away, she noticed the locket hanging around the woman's collar. Lucille caught her stare.

"This attracts you, does it? It's gold, Adele. Look! You see this? This is my dead son, for whom I mourn!" She opened the locket with trembling fingers. "Take a look at this, Adele." She pushed the locked in front of Adele's face. "For the disgrace of not mourning your parents, my son's spirit will curse you!"

A small image of Grai's smiling face lay under glass on one side of the gold locket. On the other, to Adele's horror, was a lock of his hair. Adele turned cold. She looked into the woman's small beady eyes, red with tears, her high cheekbones flushed, her thin lips bent in a forever frown. Adele stood and backed away.

"Our rituals and religion are our own affairs, Lucille," Aunt Eloise argued and jumped to her feet, her face flaming with anger. If

120

Lucille hadn't had a veil, her aunt might have scratched out her eyes. Adele would be happy to help if it came to that.

"Regardless of how they died, respect for the dead is fundamental. I thought you knew better." Lucille snapped her locket shut, gave Adele an evil glare, and let down her shroud.

"Mourning rituals are for Easterners and the British, and those who don't look for better days," Aunt Eloise said.

"You disgust me, Eloise. You and your free thinking. I've never liked you much. I've a mind to tell Richard to take me home."

"If you do, make sure you tell him why," Adele said.

Both of the women looked at her.

"What did you say?" Lucille tossed her head, indignant.

"It's not fair to condemn Aunt Eloise by judging her according to your standards. She's done nothing wrong. And I refuse to accept your curses."

"Young lady, if you knew half of what you were talking about, you'd hold your tongue. If the spirits of those two murderers take refuge in this house, you'll be a pitiful sight. If anyone should bemoan the Johansson' deaths, it should be you!"

"Lucille your despondency is inhibiting your intellect!" Aunt Eloise crossed her arms, her fists clenched. She remained a lady, a virtue Adele wished her aunt would neglect for the moment.

"Is it?" Lucille retorted and pointed to the clock. "I see you did not stop time in honor of your sister. The profanity of the deceased will fall on your household."

"What is all this ruckus? Lucille!" Richard appeared in the hallway. He looked silly, holding a delicate teacup in his large hand with his mouth agape. As much as Adele hated him for hurting Grai, she was glad he interrupted his wife. "Are you offending our hostess?"

Lucille took a long, drawn-out breath and clammed.

"Sit down, woman, and don't speak to the Barringtons in such a manner again."

"I'm sorry. My misery had the better of me." Lucille crumpled like a rag doll on the couch. The melodrama was too much for Adele. She picked up Butterscotch and seated herself on the rocking chair, trembling. The lock of Grai's hair sealed behind a piece of glass hanging around his mother's neck horrified her.

"I told you it was too soon to socialize. You must excuse us, Eloise. Grai's death has overwhelmed Lucille."

Adele cringed when she heard his name and clenched her jaw, fighting the explosion inside of her.

"You would be much happier if you knew what happened to him. A decent burial would bring closure, Lucille," Aunt Eloise responded too collected for Adele's taste. But Aunt Eloise didn't know about Grai's situation.

Adele closed her eyes for a moment and when she did, an image of Grai appeared, and she heard his words. "I hope they never find me!" Adele hoped so too. She would get to see him again, and that alone comforted her—that she knew where he was, and that Lucille and Richard Bonneville did not!

"I hope they don't find you either," she whispered.

"What?" Richard Bonneville asked.

"I was talking to the cat," Adele answered without looking at him.

"We didn't come to discuss our sorrows, nor our son. Fortunately, Nicholas and I have settled our affairs, and you and I can go home, Lucille. Thank you for your hospitality, Mrs. Barrington, Nicholas!" Richard Bonneville bowed cordially to Aunt Eloise and Uncle Nicholas. To Adele, he nodded slightly, and took Lucille's arm, prodding her to the foyer where he put her coat on her, gathered his winter wear, and saw his wife to the door.

The silence that they left behind felt good. Adele glanced at her aunt, and then at her uncle. They both exhaled.

"What brought that on?" Uncle Nicholas asked.

"Her superstitions have gotten the best of her, I'm afraid. The woman gets worse every time I see her, with or without a death in the family."

Uncle Nicholas grunted and left the room.

"What did she mean about the mirror?" Adele asked.

"Lucille hangs on to the belief that a mirror can trap a spirit and keep them in our world. She claims not enough residents of Port Summerhill cover their mirrors after a death, and that's why we have so many ghosts."

Adele shuddered. "She truly believes that?"

With Butterscotch in her arms, Adele stepped up to the mirror and studied her reflection. She didn't look as gaunt as she had the first day of her arrival. In fact, it seemed she had gained a little weight. Neither was she as pale as the day they sentenced her parents. Living with Aunt Eloise made her healthier, and more attractive.

"Lucille also claims that if you are the first one to look in a mirror after a death, you will be the next to die."

Adele's eyes widened.

"It's just superstition." Her aunt had come up behind her and took her shoulders. "You look lovely. Get some sleep and don't let that woman's bitter words upset you."

Musings

Grai leveled the frozen ground with a pick and shovel, mapping out where he would begin. He set four stones to mark the corners of the foundation but after that he didn't do much more. His wound throbbed and the pain took his balance and ability to think. He retreated to the root cellar, exhausted and in pain. Once inside, he lit the lantern which flickered and then burned steadily, illuminating the walls with a soft red glow. Grai set the lamp down on the desk next to a stack of papers and stared at the blueprints he'd been working on, not with the eye of an architect, but with the eye of a man who had all but given up. Why finish mapping out a dream when it's going to be ripped out from under you?

They were good designs, articulate, and well thought out. He remembered his grandfather's manor and had drawn the same floor plan, except for a drawing-room that would receive the southern light, and a fireplace in the main bedroom. The draft for the ground floor had been completed, leaving only the upstairs and the towers. He could do the paperwork easily enough. The hard labor would be another challenge entirely. Not long ago his body was up to any task Grai needed to do. Now, even walking took the life out of him.

He collapsed on the bed next to the blankets Adele had given him, letting his fingers linger on its softness. Soft, like her touch had been. He suppressed the longing she aroused in him and huffed out a laugh, ridiculing himself for thinking he could have a relationship with a woman in his present condition. Separation from his spirit meant a total loss of compassion. Living with such damage was hard enough alone. A man trailed by a severed soul could never show his face in public, much less allow himself to be loved.

If he lived much longer with this disorder, he must live a life of solitude.

Grai spread out on the bed and let his mind slip into a vegetative state, a defense mechanism he practiced when he found himself alone, away from Grai the spirit. Not only did daydreaming keep away the agony of knowing his family wanted him dead—but helped to relieve his physical pain. The longer he sat in the dark and be inattentive, the better he could manage life. So, he stared at the shadows on the rock walls that were cast by the lantern, listened to the silence that only a dugout could imprison, and felt the heaviness of the earth embrace him. He remained there, in this asylum he created, for the entire night. The darkness not only penetrated his environment, but his soul as well.

As if such despair had the shrillness of a ship's whistle, his spirit answered the call and rushed into the root cellar, filling the chamber with warmth. He floated over the desk, studied the blueprint for a moment, and then pretended to sit on the chair.

"You didn't work on the plans again?"

"I did a little work on the foundation. I had no reason to finish the blueprints if I can't do the labor."

"Hmm," his spirit said, peering at the papers on the desk again. "I wish you had."

"Why?"

"Because it helps you look to the future."

Grai breathed a sour laugh. "What future?"

"Your future. You're alive, Grai. There's tomorrow. We can overcome this glitch that we're experiencing!"

"I'd like to know how," Grai answered him.

"Give us time. Healing."

Time and healing—two elements Grai lacked. Time will slip away. The land will be sold. Without proper care, he will never be healed. And how would he ever be fully joined with his spirit again? The longer they remained apart, the more he pushed his life force away, just as he had unintentionally scorned the woman who came to tend to his wound.

"Adele," he whispered. Somehow the darkness made it easier to see her and remember how gentle she had been, wrapping his wound while she bore a self-inflicted laceration—self-inflicted on his behalf.

"She sacrificed her blood to bring me medicine," he said aloud. "Who would do such a thing? Why?"

"Because she loves you," his spirit said.

"How could she love me? She barely knows me."

"She's getting to know your spirit quite well if I do say so," his spirit boasted. "Few people have an opportunity to meet the entire better side of a person all at once. You see, while you suffer here in pain and belligerency, I can show her your good side. When we work as a team, we have an amazing advantage, Grai."

"You showed her my arrogant side?" Grai asked. "While I treated her discourteously."

"No, I wasn't arrogant at all."

"What did you say to her?"

His spirit gave him a look of surprise, as if he didn't know if he should answer that question. When Grai returned his pretense with a snicker, the spirit succumbed.

"Oh, not much."

"Not much about what?"

"I made her a bouquet."

Grai rolled his eyes. "What are you trying to do to me?"

"I'm not trying to do anything to you. I like her, Grai. I think you do too."

Grai leaned over and buried his head in one hand and held his side with the other. Pain shot through him again. It seemed whenever something upset him, the anguish of the injury returned. He breathed deeply and gathered his thoughts. He had to make his spirit understand the gravity of their situation and stop him from treating their circumstance like a child's game!

"Her uncle might be the person behind the attack. He wants this property. He knows my stepfather. Barrington is a big name in this territory. He has the money to get anything he wants. He has the money to get people to do anything he wants."

"So now you think Barrington wants you dead?"

"He could very well have been the instigator," Grai concluded.

"I thought you said your stepfather was the instigator."

"And you told me I was wrong."

"I said you could be wrong."

"If Barrington paid to have me eliminated, and no one found my body, he might assume I came here. He could be sending Adele to find out."

"That makes no sense, Grai."

"Bonneville doesn't know I'm alive, but Adele does, and Adele lives next door with the Barringtons."

"So, now you think that Adele told him you're here."

"Yes. It's possible."

"And she nursed your wound because...?"

"I don't know. Because she is who she is," Grai answered, softening his voice. He didn't know why she nursed his wound, nor why she cut herself to locate her uncle's medicine.

"So—" The spirit pouted and fingered the etching on the desk, the one Grai made with his knife whenever he needed a moment to think.

"So, then I guess you aren't ready for me to tell you this other news," his spirit said.

"What news?"

The spirit shook his head. "It's not important."

"We can't have secrets. That's what you keep telling me. What news?"

"Adele's parents were hanged today," he began, peeking up at Grai like a timid child.

"I'm aware."

"They murdered someone."

"And?" When his spirit didn't answer, Grai leaned toward him. "Someone I know?" Grai waited.

"Professor Reinhardt."

"What? God no." Grai closed his eyes. The words hit him with the same strength as the earthquake that had toppled his grandfather's manor. A long moment passed before he could speak. How did Adele's parents even know the professor? Why did they kill him? And did the murder have anything to do with him?

If there had been anyone on this earth who Grai could ask for help with the estate, it would have been Professor Reinhardt. Even though Grai met him only a few times, his grandfather collaborated with the professor for years, spoke highly of him, and thought of the man as a brother. Now he's dead.

"So, the murder of Professor Reinhardt means the plot to steal my inheritance is more widespread than we initially thought."

"And Professor Reinhardt's apprentice, Jim Marlin Delaney, helped to murder the professor and is running free."

"Delaney? He might come after me." Grai's heart raced. "Delaney knows this place. He knows about the gold. He might even have a map to this dugout. Maybe he was one of the men who had tried to kill me."

"Maybe so, but Adele had nothing to do with it," his spirit assured him. "Nothing."

"This she told you, I assume?"

"How could she have been involved? She's a pretty young thing," Grai's spirit defended.

"Why are you so naïve? Who made you that way? Surely not I!"

"There are some people in this world who are trustworthy."

"And you know who these people are? By what means?" Grai stood, holding his wound, and paced across the tiny room, kicking at the bag of gold he nearly stumbled over.

"I can feel it."

"You can feel it? If you are so sure who can be trusted, why are we in this condition? Why do I have this cut up the side of my belly? Why was I strangled until I couldn't breathe? Why did I almost die? If you can feel who is trustworthy, then why didn't you in the first place?"

"I'm sorry about those things," his spirit apologized, with no other explanation.

"And so, you gave this woman a bouquet. Because you 'feel' her innocence. Because she's a pretty young thing and you're attracted to her. You probably romanced her as well."

His spirit raised a brow, shrugged, and smiled.

"You were out there a long time, weren't you? All day? What were you doing?"

"Waiting."

"For what?"

"Mostly for her to stop crying."

Grai hadn't expected that. Of course, she'd cry. Her parents were hanged this afternoon. Like a cold and heartless brute, he had rebuked her during her crisis while his spirit had shown her compassion. Grai fell back on the bed.

"You're a better man than I," he whispered.

"Nonsense. I am you."

"I just don't want you losing your heart to this woman."

"I won't. It will be your heart."

Grai wiped his face with his hands and shook his head. What does one do with an impossible spirit?

"We don't know her," he tried to explain. "We have to treat everyone as a suspect."

"Until?"

"Until we find the people who want us dead."

"Ah! There is the crux. Until we find these conspirators, everyone is suspect. Even pretty young ladies who give us blankets and nurture our wounds. Does that really make sense, Grai?"

Grai shook his head and relented.

"No."

"Murderers don't repair bodies, they destroy them. Adele is not a murderer."

Grai nodded. Had he gone into his depression so deeply that he wanted Adele to be the enemy so that he could deny his affection toward her? Whatever darkness lay in wait for him couldn't include her. She'd been kind, thoughtful, sacrificing. She would have already killed him if it had been her intent.

"You see it my way then?"

"What else can we do?" Grai asked.

"Let Adele be your eyes and ears. She offered to help. Agree to her offer."

"It's too risky."

"Grai, my man, what other choice do you have? To sit here in the dark forever, hoping the murderer will return to finish us off. And then what? How will you protect yourself if that happens?"

"I have my grandfather's rifle."

His spirit shook his head.

"Trust Adele. She means well for you."

"Is that all?" Grai asked his spirit, ready to be rid of him again.

"That's all I know."

The wick on the lantern had burned to ash and would soon be out. "What time is it?" Grai asked.

"Morning. You brooded all night."

He tossed the covers aside and staggered to the hall.

"I need fresh air."

As he stepped outside and breathed in the morning's cold, his mind became clearer. Already his wound had begun to heal from the salve that Adele had applied. He didn't feel as though he would die any minute, at least. But the bandaged needed changing, and he hoped Adele would return with more ointment.

Voices came from where the Barrington's stables were located at the southern edge of the Madison's property along an access road that bordered the furthest most point of Grai's estate. When Nicholas Barrington's coachmen drove the carriage up the hill, Grai heard the team of horses. Curious, he staggered along the frosty trail to the gate where he could watch from afar. His spirit followed him.

"I'm assuming your mind has changed then and that you no longer believe Adele engaged in Reinhardt's murder?" his spirit asked.

"If she had been involved, she would have been executed with her parents," Grai answered as the carriage pulled to a stop in front of the Barrington mansion.

"You surprise me."

Grai snickered and raised a brow. "I surprise my own spirit?"

"Sometimes. I didn't know I would be so successful with her defense. I was ready to take you on at all costs."

Grai laughed and held his breath, his attention less on arguing with his spirit than on Nicholas Barrington. The man stepped out of his house dressed in a top hat and stylish frock. He said something to the coachman and returned to the manor.

"They're going out," Grai mumbled, his eyes peeled to the scene, remembering Adele had told him about the event happening today. Sadly, Adele would not be visiting him.

"You miss her already, don't you?" the transparent tormentor whispered in his ear.

"Any affection you see in me is simply a response to the kindness that she's given me," Grai argued, knowing it was a lie. "Anyone would yearn for such affection. I'm only human. Besides, my dressing needs changing."

"Yes, I see," his spirit responded.

Not until Grai saw Adele appear did his heart stammer. He didn't recognize her at first with her hair braided and tucked under a flamboyant bonnet. She wore a dark stole, expensive fur. Her skirt glistened in the sunlight, a pale green silk. When she turned around to speak to her aunt, though too far away to see her face, her beauty sent a dull pain to his heart. He swallowed.

"You are lonely, aren't you?" his spirit asked.

"Lonely? With you badgering me constantly. That's near impossible."

"For a woman."

Grai sighed. He couldn't fool himself.

"I would that I could live a normal life. Forget about adversaries and their threats of murder. I would that I could return to my apartment, make this wound go away and all the pain with it, clean up and dress properly. I would court that woman as a gentleman ought."

"Mm," his spirit agreed. "They're going to some sort of function. Pray there are no other gentlemen there who take an interest in her."

"Why?" Grai turned around and grimaced at his spirit. "Why would I deny her a healthy relationship with someone? She's had pain and grief of her own. The agony the poor woman is going through is worse than mine. She deserves to be happy." Grai swallowed the ache of seeing her step into the coach. It might be the last time, especially if she meets a young suitor of status. Her aunt and uncle would want to marry her off quickly. Less of a burden for them. "I can't give her happiness. What do I have to give anyone but a smelly dugout and a toppled foundation to a house that may never stand again—and the threat of her being murdered next to me?"

"Come now, Grai. You're not giving up, are you?"

"Giving up? Giving what up? I hardly know the woman."

"And yet you love her."

"Nonsense," Grai argued. His spirit only raised his brow.

"I have nothing to give up. Except for my life."

"And I'm not letting you relinquish such a valuable commodity at the moment."

Grai turned again to watch the Barringtons. With Adele and her aunt inside the carriage, Nicholas climbed onto the seat next to the coachmen. With a gentle "yah" the horses trotted down the drive. Grai watched until he could no longer see them, until their absence left him empty inside.

Revelry

Instead of the mules, which Uncle Nicholas used for long-distance travel, he had the coachmen harness two of his finest horses to the carriage. Uncle Nicholas would oversee the festivities and Aunt Eloise was to greet the out-of-town guests, so they left early. With a clear sky and frosty air, Adele, wrapped in a winter fur belonging to Aunt Eloise, and a lovely bonnet Lila had purchased for her, stepped into the carriage. Despite the cold, Uncle Nicholas rode outside with Mr. Fernsworth while Aunt Eloise gave Adele last minute instructions.

"What does it matter where my pinkie is when I sip tea?" Adele asked.

"It matters because it matters. People will watch everything you do. It's just what happens at these events. Especially for a new young lady coming out into the world."

"What people are watching me?"

"Everyone, Adele."

"Why would they be watching me?" Adele was a country girl raised in a seaside town where no one paid attention to her. There were no notables in Port Galleon to impress. All their neighbors were as poor as her family, struggling to survive. That anyone would care to observe how she drank her tea or held her fork seemed an outlandish concept.

"Remember, I told you this was your debut?"

Adele nodded.

"Not only will young men be watching you, but their mothers and fathers will as well."

Adele rolled her eyes, sparking a frown from her aunt.

"Just be mindful of how you oversee yourself. Most importantly, don't argue. Especially not in public!" Aunt Eloise pulled back the curtain and glanced out the window as the carriage lunged forward. For someone attending a social gathering, she had a foul temperament this morning.

"This celebration means a lot to you, doesn't it?" Adele asked.

"It means a lot to my husband. He's put everything he could into convincing these men to bring the railroad up this way. He's even risked his savings. This could be the event that will tie the knot. Or cut the string. Anyone of any importance will be there, including one or two skeptics from the press. It's not a celebration, which worries me."

"Why? What would happen if they failed to get the railroad to come? Wouldn't things just go back to normal?"

"Your uncle refuses to fail, Adele."

"That's silly. Everyone fails some time or another."

Aunt Eloise looked her in the eye. "Nicholas does not fail. If this deal doesn't go through, there is no telling what he'll do to push it through. He will get his way."

Aunt Eloise made her point with such force that Adele said nothing more but sat back and let the rumble of the carriage distract her.

Adele thought of Grai and his spirit, and those thoughts brought solace to her soul. She refused to be disturbed by the confrontation with Lucille Bonneville the night before, even though the image of Grai's ringlet imprisoned in her locket upset her. No wonder Grai wanted to get away from her and Bonneville. All Lucille's weeping over Grai did nothing to gain Adele's sympathy. The woman was evil and yes; she betrayed her son.

Adele appreciated no one's company like she did Grai's. He had such a gentle spirit, loving, beholden of nature and beauty. There was no way his spirit could curse anyone. Shame on Lucille Bonneville for even suggesting such a matter! I truth, living in such a callous world, filled with murder and robbery and evil-doings, the time she spent with Grai's soul had been delightful. Even Grai, himself, as detached and hurting as he was, offered a gentleness she'd not experienced before. She regretted that she couldn't visit him today, and her heart ached over him asking her to leave. If his spirit told him about the professor, he may never want to meet with her again. Adele swore she would go to him first thing in the morning and mend their relationship, no matter the cost.

As the dirt road ended and the horses slowed, their hooves clicked a gentle rhythm on the snow. Adele peeked out the window again. Having only seen the courthouse in Port Summerhill, Adele enjoyed the festive atmosphere of the metropolis and its shops. Horse-drawn sleighs, carriages like her uncle's, and shoppers covered the wintry streets as the hands on the town clock struck noon. When they arrived at the inn, proprietors sauntered inside. Men with turned up mustaches, silky top hats, and tailored suits carried leather briefcases as they crowded into the hotel. Adele wondered if they were guests of her uncle's or simply visitors to Port Summerhill. By the manner in which Uncle Nicholas greeted them when he jumped off the carriage, shaking hands and patting shoulders, she surmised he had invited them. Though the official revelry was not scheduled until the evening hours, the hoard of people who had previously gathered were themselves the party.

"Most of these guests are from out of town," Aunt Eloise told Adele. "I will have to hustle and make certain staff is ready to feed them."

Aunt Eloise led Adele into the lobby, but there was no hustling

136

for her auntie, as men and women stopped her on her way to the kitchen. For those who knew the Barringtons, Aunt Eloise gave a cordial greeting and introduced Adele. Adele, remembering the etiquette that Aunt Eloise had instilled in her before they left, curtsied for everyone to the point of being redundant.

Her aunt forgot their original mission to check on the kitchen staff. She took Adele's arm and pulled her toward a group of people standing near the ballroom.

"It's been a lengthy time, Eloise," Mrs. Travis said and greeted her with a kiss on the cheek.

"Too long, Bell. I want you to meet my niece, Adele."

Adele curtsied, blushing while doing so as the young men by Bell's side were smiling at her. They were identical, and it didn't take long for her to realize they were twins. Bell held out her hand to Adele and squeezed it.

"We heard about your tragedy, my dear. I'm so glad you're in expert hands now. Eloise and Nicholas will treat you right."

"They've been quite hospitable and are exceedingly kind. I'm honored to meet you," Adele said.

"These are my sons, Jacob and Caleb. They're looking forward to the dance this evening." The brothers nodded, but they were as distracted by the excitement of the occasion as Adele. So many people were already inching their way into the hotel that one could barely focus. Tobacco smoke floated above everyone's head, obscuring the air. Coat racks filled up quickly with overcoats and hats while broad-shouldered men shook hands with each other and puffed on pipes. The ladies slipped away from their male counterparts into a sitting room where delicate teapots lined a table. Adele had never seen such beautiful gowns all in one place, worn by equally attractive women.

Aunt Eloise excused herself and left Adele with Mrs. Travis and her two sons in the tearoom. The woman made small talk, and Adele entertained her as best she could, but when Jacob and Caleb invited her to the refreshment table in the ballroom, Adele hastily agreed to attend them. Aunt Eloise needn't have worried about food as the hotel staff already set out a punch bowl and trays of oysters, crab, and other shellfish dishes. Jacob fixed a plate for her and Caleb brought her punch.

"We don't know most of these people in here," Caleb whispered to her.

"Neither do I," Adele said.

"That's right, you're a visitor to your Aunt and Uncle's, aren't you?" Jacob asked.

"Yes, I'm living with them.,"

"And you're from where?"

She breathed deeply, glad to know the rumors about her hadn't circulated entirely. Yet.

"Port Galleon," she replied.

"Oh," Caleb said, with an obligatory smile. "It was your parents who were…."

"We attended the—" Jacob's brother bumped his arm and spilled punch on his sleeve.

The hanging. Go on and say it! Adele thought to dare him and reconsidered. There was no need for her to be impolite.

The awkwardness of the moment brought a silence as the boys looked at each other. "I'm sorry. I didn't realize you were that niece. Well, welcome to Port Summerhill."

Adele smiled a polite "Thank You".

"Lovely dress." Jacob's face had turned beet red.

"My Aunt Eloise made it."

"If you'll excuse us, there's a family member over there whom we need to greet." Caleb pointed toward the door but didn't indicate anyone in particular. They both bowed away cordially and left Adele alone by the reception table.

It suited her fine that they refused to be seen talking to her. She abhorred small talk, and Aunt Eloise's plan to marry her off with an offspring to one of her rich friends didn't sit well with her, anyway. She'd rather pick her own mate, and not by how large his bank account or what sort of status his parents entertained. Oddly, none of the men in this room looked attractive to her. That might have been because only one man occupied her thoughts at the moment, and he hadn't been invited to this party. If he had been, he wouldn't have come, not in his present condition. She giggled at the thought of Grai's spirit trailing in behind him, smiling and waving at everyone.

The maid set out another tray of hors d'oeuvres—sweets this time—and Adele asked if she could help in the kitchen. The woman smiled and laughed, shaking her head. When the servant had finished distributing the food, she hurried away with the empty tray.

Obviously, rejection would be Adele's lot in life. She didn't mind. Wealthy people meant extraordinarily little to her. Their conversations amounted to not much more than weather prediction and gossip. Adele had nothing to say unless she could find an interesting soul who would share her love of roses blooming in hoarfrost. She doubted that would happen here. Being alone gave her the ability to slide in and out of the crowd, listen candidly to conversations as they arose, and if Benjamin appeared she could easily disappear. She already scoped out her escape route. After smiling cordially to so many individuals, her cheeks hurt, so Adele found a chair near the reception table and relaxed, admiring the elegant gowns of the women attendees. She'd never seen so much finery gathered in one place. Decorative hats topped sweeping hairdos, jewels glistening in the chandelier light dangled from ears, and delicate stones adorned swan-like necks as women smiled and fanned themselves, sending signals to available men. How very lovely! Dazzle for the eyes, pointlessness for the soul.

The chamber continued to rumble with conversations spiced with laughter. Her uncle's voice resonated above the others, perhaps because she recognized it. Uncle Nicholas stood a good two inches above most people in the room, and with his top hat on, he easily drew her attention. Dignitaries swarmed around him in their silk vests, colorful ascots, and tailored suits, as well they should. Uncle Nicholas was, after all, the host, the hotel owner, and the facilitator of this event—the man who invited the railroad to Port Summerhill to drive them all to prosperity.

One such personage shadowed Uncle Nicholas as though her uncle held the highest station in the territory. She learned from listening to his conversation with her uncle that he was the town clerk.

"We're indebted to you, Barrington. When this is completed, there will be a key position for you in politics. Perhaps the legislature will finally change our governance to mayor, and you'll be the lucky Joe."

Uncle Nicholas laughed as he strolled over to the refreshment table near her, picked up a tea cake, and plucked it on his plate.

"I'm not so sure I want to be in politics. I've my eyes set on more lucrative ambitions." Uncle Nicholas nodded a smile to Adele. A façade, of course. He would never nod a smile to her at home. He failed to introduce her though, and for that Adele sympathized with him. There was no need to introduce her to dignitaries during such an important occasion. She was the secret disgrace of the family's and even though she enjoyed wearing this elegant gown and playing the part of a respectable woman, she would have been happier at home visiting with Grai and his spirit. She sipped her punch and settled in to observe and listen.

"Bonneville! I see you came, after all!" Uncle Nicholas held out his hand to the red-headed Richard Bonneville.

Adele nearly choked on her drink. She had no desire to interact with Grai's stepdad tonight, not after what happened with his wife the night before. Adele turned her head to view the musicians as they filed into the ballroom. Two violinists and a cello. A welcome distraction! She hoped Bonneville would not approach her and say anything about Lucille, or Grai. She dared not bring attention to herself by staring at him. Still, she'd love to hear his conversation with her uncle in case they talked about the Madison property, so she remained in her chair.

"How is the Missus tonight?" Uncle Nicholas asked.

"Much better. The woman is moody, but nothing that I don't have a handle on. My deepest apologies for what happened. Lucille adheres to her unsettling superstitions. I just wish she wouldn't be so judgmental of others. Eloise has recovered?"

"Eloise is a saint," Uncle Nicholas remarked. Adele glanced at him. As crude as he can be sometimes, even to her aunt, he at least displayed respect for her in public.

"Yes, well, I wish I could say the same about my wife."

Uncle Nicholas cleared his throat, his signal to change the subject.

"It looks as though this railroad deal is going to pull through," Bonneville said, nodding at a couple who passed by.

"I'm optimistic. There are still three more bankers from San Francisco to convince, and they haven't arrived yet. I'm trusting you'll give them the blueprints for the depot and the paperwork they're looking for. Once they hear about our plans for the terminal, I don't think they can refuse us."

"Ah yes, the property," Bonneville sighed.

Adele eyed him, her cheeks flushing. They *are* going to talk about Grai's grandfather's estate!

"Like I told you last night, we're still working on it," Bonneville said.

"You gave the impression when we spoke in my quarters that the title was clear."

"Perhaps you didn't understand. The deed is almost in our hands.

141

We've done everything within our power, we have only a few things to tend to."

Adele's stomach turned. A few things? Like finding Grai's body. Suddenly she felt ill. She pulled a hankie from her purse and coughed. Uncle Nicholas glanced at her, but she stuffed the hankie back in her purse, took a sip of her punch, and picked at the food on her plate, pretending not to see him.

"We'll need a time frame, Richard. Your wife's performance holds no weight in court. I promised you I'd have the earnest money in your hands by next week. How much longer do you need?"

"The paperwork is in motion but—." The man seemed anxious and looked to the crowd for a distraction. "You know full well there's a minor detail that we can't, at the moment, resolve."

"Don't," Uncle Nicolas spoke in a near whisper. "…bother me with minor details, Richard. I don't want to know about them. You promised you'd take care of this."

Bonneville nodded, inhaling a long trembling breath. He handed Uncle Nicholas a crumbled sheet of paper and when Adele peeked, a drawing of a dark-haired man with a scar glanced back at her. "They say he's here in Port Summerhill. Two detectives came by this morning asking if we'd seen him. I thought you should know. Delaney's his name."

Uncle Nicholas studied the flyer and then folded it carefully.

"What's this to us?"

"He might lay claim to the property. He was Reinhardt's partner. They had half interest in Madison's business."

"More of a reason to get the title." Uncle Nicholas said.

"I can't yet!" Bonneville insisted.

Adele could not help but stare at the two. Bonneville walked away. Uncle Nicholas pivoted and frowned at her. Saved by Aunt Eloise summoning him, Uncle Nicholas turned his back on Adele and gave his wife his attention.

"I believe the men from San Francisco are here, Nicholas," Aunt Eloise announced.

"Very well." Uncle Nicholas headed toward the entryway, and Aunt Eloise came to Adele.

"I have someone I would like you to meet." She took Adele's hand. Adele set her cup and saucer down and followed her through the crowd.

"Auntie, maybe you don't want to introduce me to all your friends. The Travis boys couldn't get away from me fast enough when they learned I came from Port Galleon."

"Don't be silly, Adele," she argued. They headed for a middle-aged woman sitting at a table with an elderly gentleman who weighed more than his waistcoat allowed him, wore a pin-striped suit, and had his ascot untied and loose around his neck. His balding head beaded with sweat.

"This is Mary Sellers. She's Mr. Swan's personal secretary. Mr. Swan owns the Bank of Port Summerhill."

Adele curtsied. The woman wore a black dress with mutton sleeves and a tight lace collar. She had on a large bonnet with ostrich feathers that rustled over her gray hair. Adele guessed she must be forty years old, fifty, but her large brown eyes were full of life. She took Adele's hand with a soft touch.

"My dear Adele. I feel as though I've met you already, having heard so much about you."

"Oh," Adele said and looked at Aunt Eloise.

"Never you mind about what happened in Port Galleon. You're with us now, and you have no better teacher than your aunt. I just wish I had been as fortunate as you to spend time with Eloise. Has she taught you to sew yet?"

"No, not yet. But she made my dress," Adele said.

"Simply beautiful, isn't it? And the color fits well with your complexion. I'm sure she'll help you find your talents soon enough. Come and spend some time with me."

Aunt Eloise left her, and Miss Sellers nodded toward the third chair at the table. The gentleman sitting with her stood, bowed, and fetched his derby.

"I'll be taking my leave, Miss Sellers."

She nodded a cordial goodbye as Adele sat down.

"That was Mr. Gabby. He's been wanting me to dance." She looked at Adele and shook her head. "I don't dance anymore. And I am not looking for a relationship."

"Me either," Adele said, and Miss Sellers raised an eyebrow.

"That's unusual."

"I believe a relationship should happen on its own without one having to look for it."

"You're a wise young lady."

Adele shrugged and shifted in her chair.

"Thank you for coming to my table at my request. I would love to get to know you."

"Me? Why?"

"We have things in common."

Adele couldn't quite read Miss Sellers' smile. Having someone friendly among all the rejections she's been experiencing baffled her.

"What things?"

"I assume our outlook on life, for one. This situation is awkward for you at the moment." She spoke matter-of-factly, giving Adele pause. "I know about your parents. Most everyone here does. A majority of the local people at this event went to the hanging—out of curiosity, mind you, although there are others whose tastes in entertainment are gruesome—to put it mildly. Why people are so fascinated with death is beyond me."

Adele didn't look at the woman, steeling herself against the referral of her parent's execution. Instead, she kept a keen eye on the attendees. Their mannerisms seemed so pompous as if they'd been stuffed into their silks and satins and were being manipulated by a demigod who took pleasure in their discomfort, making them interact with people they'd otherwise avoid.

"I understand," Miss Sellers said.

"What do you understand?" Adele asked, displeased that the woman brought up the death of her parents. Mary Sellers' fixed her dark brown eyes on her, and she wore a sympathetic frown.

"I see people in this town scheming to get rich while others suffer. I don't doubt you sense the same adversity."

Adele wasn't sure who the woman referred to, but her words had truth in them.

"Perhaps we could talk sometime about those things," Adele suggested. "When the room is not crowded with covetousness."

"I would like that. I work at the bank. Any time you'd like to chat, feel free to visit me in my office. It's private."

"Thank you."

"I probably shouldn't be talking so freely, but in a room filled with people who want this railroad to come through, I seem to fight a losing battle."

"You oppose the rail?" Adele asked.

"I oppose the way they're going about bringing it here. My heart is saddened by what's occurred."

"What's that?"

"The railroad is notorious for taking lives. All across the country so many good, hard-working people have died. Advocates claim it's a sacrifice we must accept, yet my heart bleeds for those who must make it. As it is, this project has not even been approved and already a fine young man has died on account of it."

Adele gaped at Miss Sellers. What did she know about Grai? "Who?" she asked.

"Oh, a grandson of the man who owned property these men are conspiring to build the terminal on. Nine hundred acres. Working at the bank, I'm also a notary and oversee their paperwork. But that's classified information and I'll talk no further of it." She sighed, hurriedly drew a hankie from her purse, and wiped her nose. "It's just that the man I'm speaking of…," she shook her head. "Not one person mourns his death. Oh, of course his mother walks about in Henrietta and Melrose crepe, flaunting her sorrow to everyone she meets, but I know the woman personally and her dismal display is nothing more than a performance. She is quite relieved he's gone, and it breaks my heart. She claims her household is quiet now that there is no more friction between Grai and the boy's stepfather. Richard Bonneville—who, rumor has it, is abusive. I wonder if he didn't have a hand in the murder as he would profit the most. It seems I'm the only one who cares. Grai Madison was like a son to me."

"I'm sorry," Adele said, biting her lip to hold her tears back. She secretly wanted to tell this woman that Grai was still alive—partially alive, at least. But that would be foolish. Wicked men are looking for him and would kill him if they knew. It seems any person in this ballroom could be responsible for his murder.

"But why are you confiding in me, a complete stranger to you?"

"Oh, you're not a complete stranger. I know your aunt and uncle well. I had a question for you concerning the professor."

"I know nothing about the professor."

"Did your parents ever bring any documents, any maps home with them the night of the crime? Anything that might appear to be a survey?"

"I saw no papers of any kind. You'd have to ask my uncle. He cleaned everything out of the house before we left. Why?"

"Just wondering. I'm a notary and work with the bankers and landowners of properties in the area. We need certain documents to show Northern Pacific. Since the professor was a business partner of Cyrus Madison, we believe he had assessment documents for that estate. If you could ask your uncle…."

Adele shrugged "Why don't you ask him? I can't help you."

"I will. I just thought since they were your parents who…oh, never mind. It's not important. I didn't mean to upset you. I can imagine what it's like for you. Please pardon me," Mary Sellers sighed and watched the attendees who were now positioning themselves to dance. "In a way, Adele, I identify with you. We both are experiencing similar heartaches—you mourn for your parents, whom the town has delighted in executing, and I mourn for young Mr. Madison, whose death the entire town celebrates."

Adele leaned back in her chair. Suddenly the elegance of the evening lost whatever glamour it could have claimed.

Miss Sellers huffed as she sat up straight and chuckled softly. "There, my dear, don't take my words so seriously. I was simply ranting. The real reason I had your aunt bring you over is to introduce you to my son. Matt Sellers." She nodded toward a young red-haired man standing against the wall, watching the musicians as they tuned their instruments.

"He would love a dance with you. I'm sure if you stood next to him he'd ask you."

Adele blushed. She never danced before, but she didn't want to disappoint this benevolent woman who was also a good friend of her auntie's.

"I'm afraid I'm not much of a dancer."

"Between you and me, I don't think he is either." Mary Sellers picked up her fan and as she waved it gently in front of her, she smiled as Matt walked toward them.

"Mother, who is this charming young lady sitting with you if I

147

might be so bold."

"This is Eloise's niece, Adele. Adele, my son Matt."

"It's nice meeting you, Matt."

His bright red hair fell over his forehead when he bowed, and his reddish-brown eyes locked onto hers. He had freckles and a pleasant smile. "Might I ask you for a dance?"

"Oh, I don't know." She shook her head, but Matt straightened and offered his hand. Adele frowned at Miss Sellers, but she saw no sense in being rude to either of them, so she accepted his hand and walked with him onto the dance floor.

There was nothing to learn. Couples bowed and curtsied and promenaded from one end of the floor to the other and repeated the formation. Though she was nervous at first, dancing amid all the lovely silk gowns, the gilded hues of the room, and dazzle of the chandeliers, the jewels on the ladies' dresses, in their hair, and on their wrists, all glittering with the rhythm of the music, she soon lost herself in the moment. For once in a long time, she found a genuine smile. Matt must have thought her pleasure was on his account, for there was a gleam in his eye when he looked at her.

Applause followed, and Adele curtsied to Matt.

"Thank you. That was pleasant."

"I hope to partake another dance with you, again?" he asked.

Adele smiled but didn't accept. He was too aggressive, and she wasn't interested in encouraging a relationship with him. In truth, she couldn't get her mind off of Grai.

"Or perhaps if you don't enjoy dancing, we might take a ride sometime. Chaperoned, of course."

Adele smiled sweetly. "No but thank you anyway." She didn't expect him to frown and grumble under his breath. Because of his reaction, she excused herself and hurried to the powder room. Aunt Eloise called from the crowd and inched through the assembly of people who stood between them. She took Adele's arm and maneuvered her to a quiet nook under the hotel stairs.

"The man you were dancing with, Mary Seller's son, did he speak to you?"

"Only briefly."

"Please be careful around him."

"He wanted me to go riding with him."

"No! Oh heavens, no!" Aunt Eloise took her hands as if to emphasize her rebuff.

"Fear not, Auntie, I refused."

"One dance is fine. Anymore and you'll be suggesting you would like to see him again."

"Is he dangerous?"

"No, not dangerous, but not husband material either."

"I'm sorry, Auntie, I wasn't thinking of marrying him simply because he asked me to dance." She laughed, her gaze caught by a woman wearing a powder blue dress and pearls. With blond hair swept atop her head in waves and curls and fastened with a hairpiece that would match a queen's. Who are these people, she wondered?

"Why does it matter so much who I dance with?"

"Who you speak with and who you dance with matters, Adele. And how many dances you accept also matters. Gentlemen are testing the waters at these affairs. Especially since this is your debut. Marriage is on everyone's minds and Matt Sellers has nothing to offer you."

"Why do you say that?"

"He was born illegitimately. He has no inheritance. Remember what I told you?"

"That you're looking out for my best interest?"

"Yes. Good, I'm pleased you remembered. Enjoy the party, and if you have questions about anyone, come and seek me out."

A friend waved for Aunt Eloise, and so that was the end of their conversation.

The hotel swarmed with people, and the temperature inside had risen. No wonder all the ladies had fans! Adele found a cool spot by a window away from the crowd and looked out over the snowy streets and at the stars. It could have been exhaustion and the heat that gave her insides an unsettled feeling, but she knew this discomfort was not from anything physical. It began during her conversation with Mary Sellers. The woman's words stirred unrest within her, and Miss Sellers had quickly obscured it by introducing her son.

What was it she said?

"You mourn for your parents, whom the town has delighted in executing, and I mourn for young Mr. Madison, whose death the entire town celebrates."

Adele repeated those words under her breath. She could not change that the town enjoyed her parent's execution. It was over. They had their thrill. But she would stop the town from celebrating Grai's would-be murder.

The Root Cellars

Having lain in bed worrying the entire night, Adele woke and put on her woollies prior to sunrise. She planned to be out of the house even before Mei Ling started cooking, and so she snuck down the stairwell, tiptoed past the closed door of her aunt and uncle's bedchamber, and slipped on her boots and her coat in the foyer. From there she hurriedly gathered bread and a slice of smoked sausage from the pantry and slipped them into a basket on the buffet. The medicine bag had never been removed from its hiding place in the kitchen, so she took that with her as well.

Cold air hit her as soon as she opened the door of the storm porch. Sub-freezing temperatures stiffened her breath and chilled her cheeks. This was the coldest she'd experienced this winter. She set the bag at her feet, looped her basket of food on her arm, pulled on her gloves, and rolled her scarf over her head.

Despite the cold, a quiet beauty laced the landscape. Hoarfrost glistened with threads of gold as the sun peeked over the horizon. The silence of this new wintry dawn excited her, as did the anticipation of seeing Grai again.

The wrought-iron gate moaned as she pulled it open and dodged the icicles that hung from the honeysuckle vines above her head. She made her way through an arbor of frost to Grandfather Madison's patio as the ground crunched under her boots. The stately fountain no longer gushed freely, but the waterfall from the figure's jug had frozen in place, fixed in an immobile pool, the ripples having frozen in their wave, clear and slick, like glass. She observed the beauty of it, and of the morning, thankful for the sense of freedom being here gave her.

Not knowing if she should call Grai's name, she wandered through the patio, past the graveyard access and the broken columns that once stood as an entry to the Madison manor. She stopped in front of the ivy laden rock work she had seen him disappear into the other day, presuming it was the entrance to the shelter he stayed in.

"Grai?" she whispered outside the stone wall.

No one answered, so she spoke again.

"I brought you a peace offering. More medicine, too. And I have news."

Of course, she wouldn't hear anyone speaking from inside, and they couldn't hear her. With granite walls, sound couldn't carry. Regardless, she waited, her heart beating heavily. If his spirit were with him, he could surely see her. The ivy above her head hung low, still green, but sharpened with ice crystals on every leaf. The pillars they clung to offered a sense of security, guarding over the entrance as if they were soldiers in a queen's army. Adele understood why Grai chose this habitat as his refuge.

"Grai, I'm not going home without seeing you. Please come talk to me."

After what seemed like hours, though in reality it had only been minutes, a slit in the rock wall slowly grew wider. Half expecting his spirit to be the one that responded, it surprised her to see Grai standing there in the flesh.

His curls were tangled about his head, his clothes twisted and unsightly. Clearly, he had just woken up. But instead of an ill-tempered greeting, which she expected, he smiled.

"I assumed you were gone forever," he said.

Relieved, Adele held out her basket.

"I brought you some food."

He backed away from the entry and ushered her into his root cellar. She hesitated, shocked that he would invite her into his sanctuary he had been trying to conceal.

"I thought…" she stuttered.

"Come in. Please," he said.

She stepped cautiously into the dark and damp tunnel which smelled of musk and wet earth. He rolled the stone closed behind her, encasing her in complete darkness. Even with her eyes wide, she could see nothing until Grai struck a match and lit a lantern. He took the basket from her and led her through a narrow passage deep into a dugout under the ground. The walls of the corridor they walked through were rock—dank and cold—but the burrow opened into a chamber equivalent in design to a small den. A desk stood up against one wall and on it were stacked papers, a fountain pen, and an inkwell. Across from the counter a granite shelf protruded, taking up most of the room's space. It was long enough for a body to lie on. On the bed, the blankets that Adele had given Grai were piled in a bundle. Leather bags filled with unknown items were shoved away in the shadows.

Even though moisture condescended along the walls, the room wasn't especially cold. There was a musty human smell to the quarters, stuffy and unpleasant.

"It's wonderful to see you, Adele," a voice spoke out of the darkness. Grai's soul floated into the light of the lantern, his smile warm and pleasant, and for once Adele found the same hospitality in both Grai and his spirit.

"It's marvelous to see you both, as well," Adele said. She put the medicine bag on the ground, set her basket on the bed, and pulled out the bread and sausage. Grai's eyes lit up as she handed it to him. He had no reservations biting into it in front of her and sat on the bed in amongst his clothes, his hat, and the blankets, devouring the meat as if he hadn't eaten in months. Perhaps he hadn't. His eagerness for food brought tears to her eyes.

"You shouldn't have to live like this," she said.

He paused, food in his mouth, and looked at her.

"Finish eating," his spirit told Grai.

Grai gave him a resentful look but took another bite.

"We know we shouldn't be living like this, although Grai here sinks into a pit of depression all too often, swearing that he deserves the worst life offers," the spirit told Adele.

Grai opened his mouth to argue, his spirit pointed at him. "Let me talk," he said, and turned back to Adele. "We've been discussing ways to escape this lifestyle, but without knowing who is looking for us and what's out there, I'm afraid we haven't come up with any ideas."

"I have news that might help you decide."

"Pray, tell."

Grai leaned over and moved his coat from the desk chair, and Adele sat down.

"Well, for beginners, there's a warrant out for this Delaney fellow."

"We knew that."

"And it's rumored he came to Port Summerhill. I saw his picture. I thought maybe if I described him you could remember if he were one of your attackers."

Grai shook his head and swallowed. "The men who assaulted me wore masks. The man who strangled me and subsequently drove his knife in me had a very raspy growl. I don't think I would recognize him. It was dark and I couldn't breathe."

"This man has dark hair and a mustache."

Grai shrugged his shoulders and took a bite of bread. "It could be him, I don't know. I know who Delaney is, though I don't think I ever met him. He was an apprentice to my grandfather's partner. Therefore, he would know more about this place than others. He might even know about the dugout. He would certainly have heard about the gold."

"Gold?"

Grai swallowed and wiped his mouth with his arm. His spirit tossed him a linen cloth, which he caught and used for his hands.

"During the war, grandfather suspected that the treasury notes the government issued would not be convertible, even though they were declared legal tender. So, grandfather started collecting gold coins. He presumed that after the war we'd be back on the gold standard. What grandfather saved would be worth more than it had been when the notes were circulated. Professor Reinhardt collaborated with my grandfather, and this Delaney, being the professor's apprentice, would know there's a cache of gold somewhere. That's why he helped your parents rob and kill the professor. It's right to fear him, yes. But whether he had a hand in the initial attack on me, it's hard to say. Maybe. The timing seems off if he was with your parents when they killed Professor Reinhardt."

She sat silently, hoping she had discovered the would-be murderer.

"Why a peace offering?" Grai asked her.

"You suspected me. You thought I was…I don't know, a spy or something."

"No, I didn't." Grai laughed.

"Oh?" His spirit crossed his arms. "That's not what I heard."

"Sometimes you hear wrong," Grai told him. "The news about the professor upset me. That your parents killed him disturbed me even more. But…." He first glanced at his spirit, and then his eyes met hers.

"I was wrong to walk away from you as I did. And if I suspected you, it was because I was wrestling with my feelings toward you. After I realized how my reaction might have hurt you, I thought you would leave me forever, and I don't want that. I want you to—" he paused and sighed. "I want you to keep coming to see me."

She smiled.

"What?"

"That makes me happy Grai because I want to continue coming to see you. Although I would be much happier if I didn't have to see you in such miserable conditions."

Grai grunted and finished the last of the sausage. He wiped his hands on the rag and tossed it on the pile of clothes on the bed.

"It's not an appropriate place for a young lady, I agree. I suppose I shouldn't have brought you in here. I was hoping for a clean dressing though, and it's cold outside."

"Please don't apologize. I only meant I wish you weren't living under such conditions. It breaks my heart. You deserve much better than this."

Grai shrugged and looked away.

"Let's change that wrap." Adele unlatched the bag and pulled out her potions while Grai took off the soiled bandage. She continued talking as she poured water over a cloth to wipe his wound clean and as she applied the salves.

"The second newsworthy event that happened last night is that I met your mother and your stepfather."

Grai winced.

"Does that hurt?"

"Some. You met my mother?"

"They came to the house."

That instilled a silence that scared Adele, and she didn't quite understand the exchange between Grai and his spirit.

"Why?"

"My uncle had some kind of business to talk over with Bonneville?" His wound looked tender, red, but she couldn't tell whether it was infected or not, the light was so dim. She applied more salve. He sucked air in between his teeth and closed his eyes.

"It's very sore. I'm sorry."

"What affairs did they discuss?" he asked, his tone accusing, or the pain made it sound that way.

"I didn't hear their conversation. I was instructed to stay in the room with my mother and yours."

"And what was that like?"

Adele sighed. "Your mother has some odd beliefs."

Grai laughed. "Let me guess, she believes in ghosts." He looked at his spirit, who shrugged.

Adele sat up and looked at him, and then at his spirit. "If I don't cover my mirror, does that mean you won't leave this realm when you die and will spend your time tormenting me and my family?"

Grai's spirit shook his head. "Frankly, what you do with your mirrors has no bearing on whether I stay here. He's the only one keeping me around." He pointed to Grai. "I certainly wouldn't torment you. I like you, Adele." He winked, triggering a smile from her.

"Your mother told me…." Adele's smile lasted only a moment, as Lucille's words bothered her all night, and she had to know if they were true. She looked at Grai. "She told me because I'm not wearing my mourning apparel and lamenting over my parents that your spirit will curse me."

"Oh, Adele," his spirit said. "You don't believe that do you?"

"She carries a lock of your hair around her neck." Adele touched Grai's hair. "It scared me."

Grai took her arm and held her hand in his.

"My mother does some peculiar things, Adele. Don't be afraid of her. And don't suppose all that she says is true. She visits soothsayers

157

and spiritualists. She's gotten far deeper into the realm of the afterlife than what's good for her. I'm more concerned about my stepfather meeting with your uncle. It seems highly suspicious to me."

"I don't know what they discussed when they came to our house, but at the dance, I eavesdropped."

"And?"

"At first they made little sense, and it seemed they were talking in code. They mentioned my uncle purchasing this property. He will give your stepfather earnest money next week. He plans on using it for the railroad terminal."

Grai's reaction startled her. He let go of her arm, flew off the bed, grabbed his derby and threw it on the floor.

"Curses!"

Adele flinched at his outburst.

About to step on the already crunched topper, his spirit rushed to rescue it.

"None of that. You've a right to be angry, but we don't destroy what little we have because of your temper!"

They stared at each other for a moment and finally Grai relented, picked up the derby, reshaped it with his fist, and tossed it back on the bed.

Adele reached out to Grai and touched his hand. "Please sit back down so I can finish wrapping your wound."

She pulled out the gauze from the medicine bag, peering into the corners to see if another roll had been hidden away somewhere. There hadn't. "I don't mean to upset you. I thought you should know what they're planning."

"Of course, I should," Grai sat on the bed, brushed his hair with his hands, and pinched the bridge of his nose. "I'm sorry," he breathed. "This was my dream. Grandfather and I were going to rebuild. Make it even better than before, a refuge for people, a sanctuary. I can't stand to think of it being logged or divided into parcels."

"You don't have to defend your stand, Grai. This land is yours. No one should make plans for it but you."

Adele put the salves away and unrolled the last of the cotton wrap.

"Regardless, last night, your stepfather insisted he had to take care of details before he could sell. And my uncle said something that was…upsetting."

"What was that?"

"I'm not sure what he was referring to, but it sounded odd. He said your mother's performance will not hold up in court."

"What? What does that mean? What performance?"

"I'm not sure if they were talking about the way she is mourning, goes on wailing about your death."

Grai stared at her with a sour expression.

"They will never find me," he swore.

Adele sighed and Grai's spirit clicked his tongue.

"Hold this end," she instructed, giving him one end of the gauze. "Your stepfather kept speaking about details that prevented him from selling."

"Details such as making sure I'm dead?"

"I don't know." She put her arms around his torso as she wrapped the bandage. He relaxed when she touched him, and their eyes met briefly. A tingle raced up her spine. He had such brilliant hazel eyes.

"I hope not. Perhaps I can somehow distract him from buying the property. They said little more than that. I think they knew I was listening."

"Your uncle could be behind the attack, Adele."

She ignored that deduction even though she had similar thoughts. It was a perplexing situation if her uncle had conspired to kill him. She'd already sworn to protect Grai, and yet she depended on Uncle Nicholas and Aunt Eloise for her sustenance.

"I don't know what I'd do if he is," she whispered. "I won't ever stop helping you." When she finished wrapping the wound, she tied the end. He took her hands in his.

"Don't place yourself in jeopardy over me."

Adele couldn't stand to meet his eyes. She slipped her hands away from his and focused on the bags that were tucked away in the shadows. Her feelings for him were extremely hard to control. How appropriate could this be, hiding in a dugout with him, unchaperoned, touching his body? Perhaps she was the woman Benjamin accused her of being. And yet, even with a reputation hovering over her, she would not trade these moments for all the silken gowns in the world.

She put the lids on her jars and tucked them into the medicine bag. She had used the last of her bandages. Uncle Nicholas would be suspicious if he found out, especially since her wound had already healed.

"Where can I get more gauze?" she asked.

"The mercantile in Port Summerhill has it," Grai answered.

"I will have to get some before Uncle Nicholas sees his bag."

"My apologies for using it all," Grai said.

"Don't apologize. I'm thinking a ride into Port Summerhill would be beneficial. There's one other thing that happened last night you need to know about. I met Miss Mary Sellers."

Grai's frown cleared.

"She wanted very much to talk with me. She used the excuse of wanting information about Professor Reinhardt and said he might have a survey of your property."

"Why?"

"They need it for probate."

Grai moaned.

"It will not happen, Grai. I believe she's on your side. She said she identified with my sorrow over my parents because she felt the same way about you."

"She's a kind woman," Grai said.

"I thought so. You see? There are those of us who care, Grai. She might help you. She says she's against the railroad and all that the town is doing to get it here. If I could tell her you're still alive—,"

Grai shook his head. "She works hand in hand with the bankers."

"Let me talk to her. She could hold up the probate court somehow. She might even know who plotted to kill you."

"Even if we knew, what could we do about it?"

"She could get you a lawyer."

"Impossible."

"Why?" Adele argued. "You need one."

"Grai," his spirit protested. "You need to do something. You can't keep building on this property without securing it as your own."

"You've been building in your condition?"

"He already has half a foundation of stone laid for the house. I told him he was going to hurt himself."

"Grai, that's a lot of work,"

"I take breaks. I have to do something."

"No wonder your wound hasn't begun to seal."

Grai rose and walked away from the two of them.

"If I don't work, I'll be worse off. I cannot lie around in this tomb waiting for my killers to show up, and I cannot appear in Port Summerhill. What else is left? If I have to build this manor stone by stone alone than that's what I'll do. I am determined to restore my grandfather's estate. Adele, if you insist on telling Mary Sellers that I'm alive, go ahead but only if she can find a lawyer who won't reveal my secret. Under no circumstances is anyone else to know!

"You won't regret it!" Elated that she had his permission to help, Adele sprang off the bed and wrapped her arms around him. Grai's

161

spirit slipped inside of him and though the two flickered as they had the first time she saw them, she felt a surge of energy come from Grai, and he embraced her like no other human being ever had. She didn't want to let go.

"It feels so good to hold you," he sighed, resting his chin in her hair. "I have not been touched like this, ever." He held onto her tighter, and then he kissed her gently on her forehead.

"You don't realize how lonely you've been until someone hugs you," Adele said. "I feel the same way."

When they parted, there were tears in his eyes. She took his head in her hands, wiped his tears with her thumbs, and kissed him on his lips. He pressed closer to her, and they embraced again. Time seemed to stand still as Adele absorbed the warmth of his body, his heartbeat beating against hers, the scent of him. They kissed and as their lips sealed together; they exchanged breath with one another.

"Adele," he whispered. "Adele." As if her name were a song, he whispered it again. He fixed a lock of her hair behind her ear. "You've done more for me in these last few days than anyone has done my entire life."

"What is it that's making my heart flutter right now?" Adele asked. "I'm drawn to you. Even last night among all those people, all I could think of was you. All day I couldn't wait to come and see you."

"And I tossed all night, worried that I chased you away."

He kissed her again, and she nestled into his arms.

"How long can you stay, today?"

"No one is awake at the house. We didn't come home until late, so I assume I won't be missed for quite a while. What time is it now?" Adele asked, disoriented from the dark cellar.

He laughed quietly "I can't help you there. My timepiece was stolen the night I was attacked."

Adele drew in a sharp breath.

"Your timepiece?"

"It was my grandfather's. An heirloom. I didn't want to lose it."

"What was your grandfather's name?"

"Cyrus. Why?"

"C.M.?"

He looked at her, puzzled.

"A large red gemstone on the latch?"

"You've seen my pocket watch?"

She swallowed and nodded. "If it is yours, my cousin's son has it."

"What? How did he get it?"

From Benjamin. Benjamin may be the man who tried to kill Grai. She opened her mouth to tell him, but instead held her hand over her lips. Her heart raced so quickly she thought she'd faint. She lived in a house with a murderer. Was her entire family involved?

"Oh, Grai," she said.

"Are you ill?" Grai asked.

"Just lightheaded."

"Let's go outside and get some fresh air."

She trembled as they walked through the dark corridor. Grai snuffed the lantern before he rolled open the entryway. His spirit trailed behind them.

The fresh air helped Adele come to her senses, and with Grai's support, she managed to stagger to the bench by the fountain without fainting. Grai sat next to her and wrapped his arm around her.

"Someone in your family attacked me?" he asked.

"Peter is forever trailing my cousin Benjamin around like a shadow. He even mimics him sometimes. I saw him with a timepiece the other day and he refused to tell me where it came from, but it would make perfect sense Benjamin gave it to him, or else Peter stole it. I wish you could remember what your assailants looked like."

163

Grai rubbed her back for a moment. His spirit had slipped out of him again and the two studied each other.

"This is the cousin who had you pinned against the outside of the house the other day?"

"He tries to kiss me. He does it as a stunt. I don't know what he'd do if we were alone. He terrifies me."

"Rightly so. You're in danger, Adele. I didn't mean for you to be at risk."

"Benjamin would be a threat to me regardless of my coming here. We're both in danger and so we need to act quickly. I'll go to Mary."

"How?"

"I'll take one of my uncle's horses to Port Summerhill directly from here. Miss Sellers invited me to come and see her, so I'll use that as an excuse. I'll ask her to contact a lawyer and then I'll return home. I'm not in dire danger. Neither my uncle nor Benjamin will know what I've done. At worse, Uncle Nicholas will lock me in my room for having taken one of his horses without asking." She shrugged, thinking about his reaction should he find out. "And having been gone all day and missing a meal."

"It's unnecessary for you to take that risk, Adele. You don't have to do any more than you have already. I can walk into town and find Mary myself."

"That's too dangerous, Grai." She took his hand and clinched it. "Let me go. I can be back before nightfall."

"You need an escort. I'll go with you."

"And get shot while on the back of one of my uncle's horses? Are you daft, Grai?"

"Grai," his spirit spoke softly. "She's right."

"If you promise to ask someone, anyone, to ride with you."

"Perhaps Mr. Fernsworth will. I'll ask him."

In Grai's condition he'd never make the trip, and if he fell off his horse into the snow then where would they be? No. She'd be much quicker riding alone. Unless, of course, Mr. Fernsworth would go with her, which she doubted. He did nothing without Uncle Nicholas' permission, but Grai didn't need to know that.

Adele and Mary Sellers

Adele had no reason to return to Uncle Nicholas' manor that morning. Grai had given her directions to the bank, and it was early enough to complete her mission and return before dark. She took a footpath from the Madison property to the stables along a slope that faced the sun. Snow evaporated into the atmosphere in heaving streams of mist, heated from the mid-morning rays and, despite the wintry air that had chilled her earlier, the day held promise. She found Mr. Fernsworth outside brushing a mule. Icy puddles of melted snow surrounded the barn entrance, so her boots sank into the sludge, and she slipped. She caught herself by grabbing the spoke of an old wooden wheel leaning up against the barn door.

Mr. Fernsworth looked up from his grooming with a cheerful and friendly smile.

"Careful there, Miss Johansson. This mud's nothing for a pretty young lady as yourself to be rollicking in."

"Rollicking it is, Mr. Fernsworth! I almost fell face first." She laughed and brushed away the tiny drops of mud that had splattered on her skirt. "Beautiful day to be with the horses, isn't it?" she said, squinting into the sun.

"Yes, ma'am. Sun's out and warming the soul. How might I help you this morning?"

"I need a ride into Port Summerhill."

Mr. Fernsworth took his cap off his head and scratched the bald spot on his head. "Did Mr. Barrington authorize me to take you?"

"No."

"Well, that's good, Miss Adele. He gave me work a plenty here to do today."

"Yes, well, he said I should just take a horse and let you go on about your chores."

"He did, did he? Not a buggy?"

"No, that would be too time consuming. A horse is fine."

Mr. Fernsworth nodded, regarding her clothes.

"Sidesaddle?"

"Heavens no!" Adele declared.

"Most ladies ride with their skirts to the side, but the young 'uns sit astride. Not sure what's proper for you as I see you as a lady."

"Thank you for that, but I'm not too old to sit astride, Mr. Fernsworth. I'm not even courting yet, and I'd be much more comfortable if I knew I wouldn't slide off the saddle."

He grunted. Nothing she wore would be appropriate for sitting astride in a saddle. Adele didn't care. She had her woollies on; the skirt had ample length to keep her modest, but not too long to obstruct her feet. Her mission needed to be carried out immediately and nothing would stop her now. Going back to the house to change clothes could prove disastrous.

"I'll get the mare saddled for you."

She waited nervously as the coachman took his time inside the barn. She glanced at the horse trough, the hay wrapped in canvas sheets for winter; the tools leaning up against a shed, but her thoughts were far from the stables. They were on Grai, on his wound, and on that horrid hole he lived in. She had to get him out of there. He was too caring of a man to be treated so unfairly. Her life had become significantly more complicated since she met him. What if Benjamin had been the one who tried to kill Grai? What if her cousin found out where Grai was, or worse, that she was trying to help him? All of Benjamin's threats suddenly had new implications. If he tried to kill once, he could very well try to kill again, and she would be one of his targets, especially if he knew she was helping Grai.

Few people would miss her. Aunt Eloise would, but only for a short time, and Adele doubted the woman would wear a mourning gown on her behalf. She certainly wouldn't cover her mirrors! Uncle Nicholas would defend his son.

If Benjamin killed her, he for certain would murder Grai as well, and the two of them would lay side by side six feet under the ground somewhere beneath the imminent railroad tracks.

"She's got spirit, but she won't take off on you. Sure-footed little mare."

Mr. Fernsworth led a bright red roan to her, a cheerful color spot against the snowy background.

"Thank you. What's her name?"

"Tessie." Mr. Fernsworth handed her the reins and helped her into a sidesaddle, despite she had asked for a man's saddle.

Once atop the roan, she sighed and looked around. Grai had given her directions to the bank, but not to Port Summerhill. She had no idea which way to travel.

"Mr. Fernsworth, which is the best road to take to town?"

The man looked at her for the longest time. Puzzled? Worried? Had he never been asked directions before?

"Miss Johannsson, there's only one way into Port Summerhill." He pointed to the road, leaving the stables still covered with snow. "Turn left at the junction."

"Thank you!" She gave him a friendly salute as she left.

Port Summerhill was not a large town. There weren't over five hundred residents in all. But word had spread throughout the northwest that Washington Territory would soon become a state now that the nation had recovered from the civil war. Rumors of a future railroad brought opportunists to Port Summerhill, and the streets of the town droned with strangers. Traffic this morning, however, consisted of sailors from the merchant ships that had docked in the port. Adele couldn't help but look at the pair of mariners standing idly in front of the hardware shop. What is it about a man in a uniform that attracts the ladies? Granted their handsome blue pullover jumpers, black silk neckerchief around their neck and flat top hats on their heads were impressive, but it was the smile one of them gave her that made her giggle. She was in no formal dress to catch their eye. But a sailor spends his days at sea and very seldom does he get to romance a woman. Before he could call her over, Adele hurried to the livery stable, Tessie trotting behind her. She handed the reins to the stable boy and asked his name, promising him her uncle would pay what little was owed the next time he came to town. From there she walked to the bank, the *"red brick building with the town clock"* as Grai had described it. She cared little that her boots were muddy, and her clothes smelled like sheep. She entered the busy building and walked up to an employee—a man with a pointed mustache, bushy eyebrows, and sideburns that nearly grew into his mouth.

"I would like to see Miss Mary Sellers please."

He looked her in the eye and squinted. "Did I not see you with the Barringtons at the reception last night?"

"I was there. I didn't notice you."

"Niece?"

Adele groaned quietly to herself. "My relationship to the Barringtons is my private business, sir. I have important matters to discuss with Miss Mary Sellers."

"She has an appointment with her son in ten minutes. Does she know you're coming?"

"Yes," Adele said. In a sense, it was true. Adele had told Miss

169

Sellers that she wanted to visit. She just never said when.

The man straightened his waistcoat and came out from behind his till. "Follow me."

He led her down a long hallway. When he stopped at a door that bore Miss Seller's name, he studied her thoroughly from head to toe before he knocked, focusing the longest on her muddy boots. Adele shifted her weight.

"Is this her door?" she asked.

He cleared his throat and knocked.

"Yes," came the reply from within the room.

"A young woman is here to see you."

"Well, let her in, Jeremy."

Jeremy opened the door for Adele, gave Adele an unfriendly glare, and then left.

Miss Sellers stood as soon as Adele entered. The woman must have a fetish for black dresses, for the one she wore this morning was of the same style she had worn the night before except for the lace collar. Instead, this one had green jeweled buttons on the bodice.

"Adele! I didn't know you'd be coming so soon after our talk. Please sit down."

Adele took a seat in a large leather chair near the woman's wood stove. Behind Miss Sellers' desk, a bookcase loomed over them with tomes of every size and cover. The room even smelled like books.

"Tea?" Miss Sellers offered.

"Yes, please."

Adele regarded the treasures on the shelves as Miss Sellers poured tea for her and set it on a small, polished table next to her. What would it be like to sit comfortably by the hearth and read books all day? She never had such leisure time. She had spent her days washing her family's clothes and cleaning house, foraging for berries and shellfish, and chopping firewood, hauling water from the spring and mending.

There had been no time to read. She had taught herself when she was small with a little help from her mother. What she read had been limited, the newspaper to her father on Sundays, or selected Bible verses to her mother. Never had she opened a novel or a textbook like the ones Mary Sellers had.

"Does your uncle know you've come?"

"No. Why?"

"Because if he did, I would assume he came with you, and then we would have to converse on a strictly social level."

Adele stared at her. "What do you mean?"

"Adele, Nicholas Barrington has ears everywhere. And eyes!" She laughed and shook her head. "The man keeps memorandums on everyone."

"I came alone."

"That was brave of you."

"Brave? Why?"

"Venturing any distance by yourself could be dangerous for a young lady. The residents of Port Summerhill are good people, but we do have our share of crime."

"I assumed nothing would happen to me in broad daylight. I expect to return home well before the sun goes down."

Miss Sellers sipped her tea, but her eyes did not waver off Adele.

"What brings you to see me, other than our conversation last night?"

"I wanted to ask you if you have any idea who might have attacked Grai Madison?" She bit her lip, thinking her question crass, but Adele had little use for chatter. She ought to get straight to the point.

"No! Why?" Mary Sellers remained affected by the sudden outburst. She set her teacup on its saucer but still held it near her lips.

"I just thought working so closely with legal documents you might have some idea who would be interested in killing him. Who is a suspect and who is not?"

"Even if I had an opinion, it wouldn't be my place to speak it. As you say, I work closely with business executives. I would be in grave trouble were I to implicate anyone of murder."

"No motives?"

She laughed and set her cup and saucer down. "There's motive enough, child. I told you that last night. The railroad. Cyrus Madison's piece of property is a prime location for the terminal. Whoever owns it when the delegates come from San Francisco with a proposal will make a fortune. Grai wouldn't sell. He wanted to rebuild the estate and make it a sanctuary. He never would have permitted a train station on his property."

"So, you're saying that anyone involved with the railroad might have killed him?"

She shrugged. "I suppose that's what I'm saying."

"What does the marshal think?"

"Why, I have no idea. I never talked to him about Grai's disappearance. No one has done any investigating because they never found a body. You can't arrest anyone for murder if there's no proof a murder took place. You need a body."

"But everyone says it was murder."

"The young man has disappeared off the face of the earth. Those of us who knew him are certain he would never leave Port Summerhill without telling someone. Besides, there is some evidence of his passing."

"What evidence?"

"Adele, please."

"What did they find?"

"Why are you so interested in someone you never met?"

"I couldn't sleep. My uncle is very much involved in the railroad, and I thought he would want to know what happened. Perhaps Port Summerhill could take precautions so that no one else was hurt."

172

Miss Sellers straightened the folds on her dress.

"So, I ask again, what evidence did they find that Grai was murdered?"

"The ground where he fell was soiled with blood and personal items had fallen out of his pockets. And his briefcase, I suppose. That's what Richard…I mean, Mr. Bonneville told me. He said someone found his briefcase."

Miss Sellers stood and walked to the fireplace, holding her hands out to the fire to warm them. Adele drank her tea, making a point of not holding her pinkie out. She had thought Mary Sellers would have been more helpful, at least more sympathetic, but her manner mirrored that of everyone else's' she met at the party the night before. Adele placed her cup in its saucer on the end table and cleared her throat.

"Grai Madison is still alive."

Mary Sellers' face paled with a look of shock. She sank into a chair across from Adele. "Where?"

"I can't tell you where he is. He's deathly afraid of the men who tried to kill him. But he sent me here to ask you to find a lawyer for him—letting no one else know he's alive."

"How did you meet him?"

"I can't tell you."

Miss Sellers stared at her so long that Adele shifted and looked away.

"Is he well?"

Adele shrugged her shoulders. "He's as well as can be expected considering the trauma he went through. You and I are the only people who know. It has to be a secret aside from the lawyer. We need to find out who is behind the attack."

"Oh, Adele, this is serious. Perhaps the marshal should know?"

"No! Maybe once we have names." Adele's face flushed. She folded her hands together so as not to bring attention to her trembling.

She has a suspect—Benjamin Barrington. Too afraid to reveal her cousin's role in the would-be murder, she held her tongue.

"Grai wanted to know if you could somehow stop probate on his property or at least hold the process up. My uncle was going to give earnest money next week, and Grai is devastated. It means so much for him not to lose the estate."

"Has Grai seen anyone else?"

Adele shook her head. "No. He's hiding."

"You seem to know quite a bit about him, for someone who never met him before."

"I've talked to him."

Miss Sellers raised a brow. "I see. Well, I don't think Mr. Bonneville is ready to sell, even if it does go through probate. Your uncle is a hard man to say no to, but I think he's going to be frustrated this time. I will do what I can. Are you attempting to solve this crime on your own, young lady?"

Adele shook her head. But the woman must know she's lying.

"I would caution against it. Whoever sought to kill him would consider you a target as well if they knew you were the sleuth on the case. A young girl from Port Galleon with a past like yours would not raise much of an eyebrow should she suddenly be disposed of."

Adele frowned.

"I'll be careful no matter what I do," she responded.

"Good. I am overjoyed to know that Grai is still alive. He should have come with you to see a doctor. There are those in town who could give him the protection he deserves."

"There are…issues, Miss Sellers. Issues that he needs to tend to before he sees anyone." She couldn't tell Miss Sellers that Grai was separated from his spirit and half of him walks around like a ghost. If rumors were going to spread, that would be the one! Grai didn't need the residents of Port Summerhill terrified of him. It could trigger more people wanting to kill him!

"I could help Grai if I knew where he was, and what condition he was in."

"I'm sorry. That would have to be his decision to make, not mine."

"Very well. I will find the young man a lawyer."

"Thank you."

Adele rose. "I need to be on my way. I trust we'll be in contact perhaps before the week is up?"

"Perhaps," Miss Sellers said.

Adele nodded a goodbye, but before she left the office, Matt walked in. She nearly bumped into him when the door swung open.

"Oh!" Adele gasped.

"Mother, I didn't know you had someone in the office." He bowed and Adele gave him a formal curtsy.

"Adele was just leaving," Mary Sellers said. "Perchance, you'd like to escort her home. We can meet when you return. I fear her presence in Port Summerhill might be dangerous, and for a young lady to ride on that mountain trail back home in the snow could be hazardous."

Surprised at the suggestion, Adele shook her head. "That's all right, Miss Sellers, I have another stop to make before I leave. Besides, I don't think I'm in any danger."

"A wonderful idea, mother! Miss Johansson," Matt bowed to Adele again, ignoring her refusal. "I would enjoy the ride, and my horse is already saddled."

"I will return alone, thank you," Adele reiterated. His smile folded into a frown.

"My regrets, then. It appears your rejection of me goes well beyond the dance floor."

His response stupefied her, and she stiffened. She barely knew the man. Surely he'd been refused a dance from a stranger before.

"Please, don't take it personally. It has nothing to do with you, only that I'm not ready to go home."

"I can wait," he said. She glared, and he relented.

"Very well. As you wish." He tipped his hat.

Adele regarded them both before she strolled out of Mary Seller's office, satisfied with what she had accomplished with Miss Sellers and perturbed at her son for being so crude.

She quickly forgot him once she left the bank and stepped in the frosty morning air. Her mind spun in various directions, contemplating what her next steps should be and who she should talk to if anyone. Since she was in Port Summerhill already, it seemed favorable to visit the marshal.

Adele had met Marshal Carry at the reception, introduced by her uncle. They had spoken briefly but the fact that he was a law officer, and she the daughter of felons who'd been hanged in Port Summerhill made their conversation awkward. Adele took a deep breath.

The quiet, good-looking man rose cordially when she walked into the jailhouse.

"Miss Johansson, I'm surprised to see you here."

"Good morning, Marshal."

"There's no sort of trouble, is there?"

"No, not exactly, sir," she said. "I just had some questions that I thought you might be able to answer."

The marshal gave her a bewildered frown and peered out the window. "You came into town alone?"

"Yes. Why?"

"It's not a safe thing for you to do." His face turned red as he offered her a seat. "I don't mean to offend you, but there are some folks who witnessed the hanging. There's talk around town and many of the newsmongers have negative opinions of your family."

"Of me?"

"Well, it would seem that way. You'd be safer having an escort."

"Thank you for the advice." She sat across from him and folded her hands on her lap, not certain how she should begin.

"What can I do for you?" he asked.

"I was wondering if you have been investigating the murder of Grai Madison."

After speaking, she realized how out of place her inquiry must seem. She wasn't supposed to have known Grai. The attempted murder happened before she arrived in Port Summerhill. She may have just made another bloomer and Marshal Carry's gawk confirmed it.

"What do you know about Grai Madison?" he asked.

"Nothing. But I think there's a link to him and the man my parents killed, and I just wondered if you have any suspects, or if you know who his murderer is."

"Grai's body was never found. You can't investigate a murder if no one was murdered. I'm curious to know why you're asking about him, Miss Johansson."

Adele stared at him wide-eyed, realizing she opened the door to being a suspect herself.

"I…I just heard the story about him from Mary Sellers and was mortified by his demise."

"We don't know what happened to him."

"No, I suppose you're right." She stood to leave. She'd made enough of a fool of herself.

"You're correct, however," he said before she made it to the door. "There is a link between the man your parents murdered and Grai's family, and the property for that matter. As you know from the trial, one of Professor Reinhardt's murderers Delaney is connected to Cyrus Madison, Grai's grandfather. Delaney is still at large. He's a dangerous criminal, Miss Johansson. I suggest you not ask any more questions concerning Grai Madison or the Madison estate unless you have an escort with a firearm."

"Thank you for the warning, and for listening. I'm headed home now. And I will take your advice and not come into town alone again."

He stood with her, gentlemen are supposed to do that sort of thing, but he didn't see her to the door. He seemed too stunned at her presence.

As soon as she walked outside, her stomach churned. She'd been too bold today, she feared, and the warning from both the marshal and Miss Sellers made her sweat. She'd like to leave town immediately, but she had one more stop.

There were no more handsome sailors on the street to distract her, and a cloud cover darkened the sky. It would snow again soon so she hurried to her next destination. As she walked past the shops along the boardwalk, she secretly wished Aunt Eloise had accompanied her.

Adele would have enjoyed being in town had she not snuck away. There were lovely items for sale in the mercantile window, though she had to avoid looking at the hand-carved casket exhibit. She'd had enough of death. The pickle barrel tempted her, and the rolls of cheeses reminded her she hadn't eaten. She decided to purchase a bite of food on her uncle's tab before she went home—a sausage and some penny-candy to suck on for the ride. As she entered the shop, the wood floor creaked under her boots. A pot-belly stove rumbled with heat, a cat jumped from a chair next to it, and a bald man stepped out from the back room.

"How might I help you, Miss?" he asked.

"I thought perhaps I could put a bite of food on my uncle's tab this morning before my ride home. Not much, if it's all right with you."

"Hm, well, that depends on who your uncle is."

"Mr. Nicholas Barrington."

The man waved and laughed. "No problem there. He's one of my best customers, always pays on time. Pick what you want."

Before Adele scouted through the food bins, she pulled a box of gauze from the shelf and placed it on the counter. She thought twice and then grabbed another and stacked it on top of the first box. As she considered which cheese she should buy, or whether to purchase a pretzel, she noticed Matt outside the shop talking to a man. She thought nothing of it when Matt walked away. The man he had spoken to entered the shop, but with his high collar frock and low sitting cap, and the sun behind him, she barely could tell what he looked like. He watched her. His gaze fell to the gauze she had placed on the counter, and then he strolled to the rear of the store, browsing through the farm tools by the back door. She thought little of him until after the merchant recorded her purchase, and she went outside and walked toward the stables. Boots resounded on the boardwalk shortly after she left the mercantile and steady footsteps remained a few feet behind her on the way to the livery. She glanced over her shoulder before she entered the barn and saw him leaning against the door. When she mounted Tessie, the man also saddled a horse.

Foolish fears. Mary Seller's words simply made her mistrustful. She had no reason to be afraid of anyone in Port Summerhill. Very few people even knew her, and those who did were friends of her uncle's. Who would do her harm? It was merely a coincidence that Marshal Carry gave her the same warning as Miss Sellers. They were concerned citizens looking out after her.

She found the trail home easy enough, and by the time she got beyond town, past the last country cottage, the sky had darkened. A winter chill seeped through her woolen coat. Limbs of fir laden with snow hung low over the trail, and the tracks her horse had made that morning were swept clean by drifting winds. Snow fell again, and poor Tessie plodded uphill with an audible wheeze. Adele was fine taking her time—despite the cold, she had enough garments on to keep her protected from frostbite. Still, the day dimmed quicker than she would have liked, so she kept a sharp eye out for the junction, not sure how soon she'd arrive. If she passed the crossroads, she had no idea where the trail she was on would take her.

Out of angst, she glanced over her shoulder. That couldn't be someone following her, could it? Her heart leaped to her throat, and she made a clicking sound to Tessie. The horse lifted her head and twitched her ears but did not speed up. Adele looked over her shoulder again. The man rode a large black horse with long legs that carried him with a quick stride. He'd be at her side in minutes. There was a chance he had been sent by Mary Sellers as an escort since Matt had been talking to him. It seemed odd though to send a stranger to follow her like this with no word, and so Adele doubted her conjecture.

"Come, Tessie, let's hurry and get you some oats," she whispered in the horse's ears. Tessie responded with only a head toss, so Adele nudged her with her knees. For a few moments, the horse took a quicker gait but soon slowed again. Adele sighed. It was already too late. The man's long-legged steed moved quickly, and she could hear him breathing now. He trotted behind her.

"Stop," he called.

Bundled up in a winter frock, his cap pulled low over his head and a scarf wrapped over his face covering his nose, his disguise prevented her from identifying him, not that she knew many people from Port Summerhill.

When she didn't stop, he trotted his horse up to her and pulled her reins. Tessie halted.

"Who are you? What do you want?" Adele yanked the reins from his hands, but he held on to them.

"Where is he?" The man had brown eyes, squinted angrily at her, and his voice was muffled from the bandana over his mouth.

"Who?"

"Don't play ignorant, woman. I can follow you and find him myself, or you can tell me where he's hiding and stay out of the way."

"Let go of my horse!" Adele demanded, pulling on the reins again. If she had a more energetic steed, she'd simply gallop away, but Tessie wouldn't exert herself.

"You're going to find yourself bloodied and in a ditch, woman," he said. "What's going on in Port Summerhill is no business of yours. No one wants to hurt you, but they will if you keep snooping around."

"I have no idea what you're talking about."

He laughed. "You make a lousy liar. Tell me where he is."

"Who?"

"Grai Madison."

She swallowed the lump in her throat, and her cheeks flushed as if she had a fever. She tried not to show it.

"I don't know who that is."

"Who's the gauze for woman?"

"It's none of your business. But if you must know, I'm taking it to my uncle."

He laughed a gruff and cynical laugh. "Right. It doesn't matter. Now that we know he's alive, it'll be easy enough to find him. Especially with a fool girl like yourself leading the way."

The man glanced up ahead, released her reins, and when Adele prodded Tessie onward, he stayed behind—and watched.

She would not go directly to Grai today.

Night Garden

When Adele returned Tessie to the stables, Mr. Fernsworth wasn't there, but another young stable hand took the horse from her without a word. She pulled her purchases from the saddlebag and hiked up the hill, deep in thought. Glancing back the way she had come, beyond the snowy road and frosty landscape that now dimmed with late afternoon darkness, nothing stirred. Still, the inescapable glare of that stranger had buried itself in her mind, and she shuddered.

Adele had left the medicine bag with Grai that afternoon. Too fearful to retrieve it, she also worried that if her uncle found it missing, she'd be in a world of hurt—not as much as Grai would be if the stranger followed her to his hideout. As she passed the footpath to the Madison estate, she avoided looking that way. It hurt her heart to do so.

The sun had near set by the time Adele reached the house. With a soiled skirt, damp coat, and wet hair, she entered through the kitchen again. Mei Ling was nowhere to be found, the stove cold, and kitchen empty. Adele stomped the snow off her boots, hung her coat on the rack in the storm porch, and entered the living quarters. Uncle Nicholas was alone in the living room waiting for her. He stood immediately.

"There's no need to tell me where you've been. I already know," he said. "Where is my medicine bag?"

"I…I borrowed it for my cut. I'll go get it." She turned to exit, but his commanding voice stopped her.

"No. Not now. Sit."

She faced him but didn't respond.

"I said sit!"

Adele meandered to the couch and, with as much grace as she could manage, sat down.

"I hear you've accused Benjamin of predatory advances. How dare you! How dare you implicate my son in such a way?"

Adele had nothing to say. She knew he'd be irate over such allegations, and she wished Aunt Eloise had kept it between them. But then, being married to someone like Uncle Nicholas, there'd be no secrets between husband and wife, at least not on her aunt's part.

"I'm going to leave that contention for another time. You will pay for it, but I mean to interrogate you both together. Benjamin needs to know about your poison. A woman can be a snake, and I have no doubt the power of your venom. You will not be using it against my son." He lifted his chin and took a breath while Adele shuddered.

Benjamin will lie, and then he'll hurt her the next time they're alone. If only Aunt Eloise had said nothing.

"That is only one grievance I have against you."

"And the other?" Adele asked.

"The others?" he snickered. "You took one of my horses from the stables this morning."

"Mr. Fernsworth saddled her for me."

"And you lied to him saying I gave you permission."

Adele fidgeted with her dress. "I'm sorry for not telling you."

"If you merely wanted to go for a ride, you could have asked. Lying benefits no one. But that is the lesser of my worries. Lila's necklace was found in your room."

"What?"

"I'm not a fool, Adele. I've been wise to your shenanigans from the moment I walked into your parent's shanty and packed your trunk.

Your family's name is in itself wicked. How your aunt ever survived the squalor of your bloodline is beyond me, save for the fact that I married her before the taint could spread. Once Lila finds out about her necklace, she will press charges, and you will be incarcerated. At that time, the Barringtons will be rid of you and your family's bane!"

"I did not steal…"

"Not a word. I have proof and I don't need you to lie to me on top of it. I'm setting those matters aside for now. I have a greater concern for the moment. What is this story my grandchildren are telling me?" He clasped his hands behind his back and paced in front of her with an alarming presence.

Adele took a deep breath, gathering her senses. How did Lila's necklace get in her room? And what did the children tell him? She honestly had no idea what her uncle referred to. "What story is that?"

"Magic in the garden. Beyond the gate. What wild tales are you telling them? Why do you even go beyond the gate? That's not our property. You're forbidden to go there."

"I didn't know, sir. And I haven't told your grandchildren any stories at all."

"No? The stories they're repeating are much too advanced for them to fabricate on their own. Especially Peter. Normally the boy would laugh at Maggie, but he rattles on about the same thing she does."

Adele shook her head. He stopped in front of her, feet spread military fashion. Adele swallowed and a cold sweat formed on her brow.

"Rainbows in the garden? Spirits floating around the backyard? Do these stories have anything to do with disappearing jewelry?"

"I didn't steal Lila's necklace."

"Now they say they heard you talking in the garden. To whom? Who are you meeting out there? Are you talking to yourself? Or do you have a partner scrutinizing our property?"

Adele's entire body turned stiff.

"I'm not a thief."

"No? It's my experience that the chips do not fall far from the block, Adele. Your parents were thieves. They murdered someone while robbing him. He was an upstanding citizen. A professor, and yet they had no regard for the man's place in life. Is that your plan as well? To murder my family and steal everything we own?"

"That's absurd."

"I knew this was dangerous, bringing you here."

Adele stood. "I'm not a thief. I would never hurt you or Aunt Eloise or Lila or anyone in this family. I'm devastated that you would think that!"

"If it upsets you so much, then tell me what you've been doing. Because as long as you lie, I will think the worse of you."

Adele trembled, the lie shifting like vomit in her throat. But she couldn't come completely clean, not without telling him about Grai. And then what would he do? What would Grai do? She wanted her uncle's trust, but she couldn't earn it. Not now. Not as long as a murderer still sought to kill Grai. For all she knew, Uncle Nicholas could have started the assault, with Benjamin being the one who carried it out.

"The truth is, I stole nothing. I have no idea how Lila's necklace got in my room, and I left your bag outside by accident. I'm sorry. I'll go get it."

"Who is out there, Adele?"

"No one!" She whirled about.

"Don't step foot out of this house. Go to your room. You will fall in line like everyone else in this family or you'll be sent to the asylum before I can blink an eye. Go!"

She turned to him. *Asylum?* Her eyes burned with tears.

"Yes. Asylum. Your aunt seems to think you're overwhelmed with grief and have no idea what you're doing. There's a place for people who can't think properly. It would take no effort on my part to take you there. Go to your room. Now!"

Adele drifted to the stairs as her uncle stormed into the foyer. She stopped midway, her heart pounding as she watched her uncle put his coat and his boots on, grab his gloves and hat and take his rifle out of the gun case.

"Nicholas," Aunt Eloise called him from the hall. "What are you doing, Nick?"

"I'm going to find a trespasser." Uncle Nicholas looked up at Adele and pointed. "Go to your room!"

To avoid bursting into tears in front of him, Adele raced up the stairs to her tower, slammed the door, and pulled open the curtain to her window.

Night had fallen, the garden had grown dark but for a gas lamp that someone had lit before sunset. Uncle Nicholas hurried through the snow bundled in his thick wool coat, his hat tipped low over his head and the rifle resting on his shoulder. He marched confidently toward the gate. Soon he disappeared into the shadows.

Adele waited by the window, hoping not to see the light of Grai's spirit. Hoping the two of them were tucked safely in the root cellar and would not come out. She watched until her eyes grew weary. No sound, no movement disturbed the evening. She paced the room and flinched when Butterscotch jumped from the desk onto the floor. Adele walked to the door and let the cat out. Even the house had fallen silent. The lanterns in the hallway had been snuffed and only one small oil lamp remained lit at the bottom of the stairs. Perhaps Uncle Nicholas had come back in through another entrance and she hadn't seen him.

She withdrew to her bed, still not ready to change into her nightclothes. Pacing and worrying at night was nothing new to Adele. How often had this been her requiem as a child in Port Galleon? Worrying and wondering when her parents were going to come home. She never felt safe until her parents walked in the door. Ultimately, her security had never been a reality. There was no safe place which she could call home. The cottage in Port Galleon had been a façade, a smokescreen for the evil her folks partook in, and she, being a child, had no idea what they'd been up to.

Tonight, those same memories haunted her. She lived identical to the way her parents had lived—lying, hiding, sneaking, her secrets consumed her in the same way. Uncle Nicholas could be right. Perhaps her deceptive lifestyle would take her to the gallows—or the asylum. These lies were all because of Grai. She had never agonized over someone like this before. Even her parents' death did not give her nausea and cause her head to spin. If Uncle Nicholas kills Grai, she will never forgive him. If Grai dies, she will never forgive herself.

The sound of a gunshot made her jump. And then another.

Adele gasped, leaped out of bed, and raced to the window. She saw nothing and assumed her uncle had been on the Madison's property when he fired the gun.

"No. No!" She moaned and then screamed. "No, please don't!" She bit her knuckles, stormed through her room, grabbed her knapsack, and ran down the stairwell. Her aunt had already rushed to the foyer to don her coat, slip on her boots, and race out the door. Adele followed,

"Eloise," her uncle called from somewhere in the dark. "Come quickly. I think I've shot a man."

She heard someone moaning, and Nicholas's voice echoed through the woods.

Adele trailed after her aunt, putting her coat on as she ran. Aunt Eloise slid on the ice and fell, landing on a cushion of bustle. Adele rushed to her and helped her up.

"Where is the medicine bag?" Aunt Eloise asked as she brushed the snow off her dress.

"It's on the bench next door. Are you all right?"

"Next door? What in the name of Lincoln is it doing there?"

Aunt Eloise's glare lasted only a second, interrupted by Uncle Nicholas calling again.

"Eloise! Hurry!"

"Where is he?" her aunt asked in disgust.

"Come this way." Adele held on to her arm so she didn't slip again. Snow illuminated by starlight guided them, but the shadows of the foliage were so dense she had to follow the vines to find the gate. When she did, she pushed the honeysuckle aside to help her aunt through.

"Why in heaven's name do you know about this gate and this property? What have you been doing, Adele?"

Adele led her aunt on the trail, now completely in shadow. Even the hoarfrost reflected no starlight. Soon they heard men talking angrily with one another. Adele bit her lip, tears leaking out of her eyes and chilling her cheeks, certain she'd find Grai wounded or dying.

They came to the patio where Uncle Nicholas leaned over someone on the ground. Another man stood behind them.

"Benjamin!" Aunt Eloise gasped.

"What I want to know is what you're doing here with this criminal!" Uncle Nicholas asked his son.

Adele had never heard her uncle raise his voice to Benjamin in such a manner, worse than when he sent her to her room. Her uncle shook his fist and trembled with rage. Surely he would have torn into Benjamin if he hadn't been holding the man he shot on the ground with his knee.

Adele immediately raced to the bench where she had left the medicine bag and brought it to her uncle. Aunt Eloise took the bag from her and rummaged through it.

"The dressings are almost gone." She looked at Adele in shock. "What did you do with them?"

"I have more," Adele had brought her knapsack for this very moment and pulled out the newly gained box of gauze. She almost grabbed the other but thought better of it.

"Why is that here?" Uncle Nicholas asked her in the same tone he'd been addressing his son. "You've been meeting this man on the sly?"

Adele stared at the man grappling belly down in the snow. Blood pooled around his leg. It clearly was not Grai. If she wasn't mistaken, it was the same man who had followed her this afternoon.

"Who is he?" Adele asked.

"I thought you would know Adele. His name is Jim Marlin Delaney. He's the man who helped your parents kill the professor."

Uncle Nicholas grabbed the gauze out of her hand. After tying Delaney's hands with a strip, he rolled the man over, pulled up his pant leg, and wrapped the wound.

"Someone needs to go to the stables. Eloise? You're the only one I can trust."

"Of course, Nicholas," she answered.

"Have Fernsworth harness the horses and bring the carriage up here. I'll take Delaney to the marshal."

When he had finished tending to Delaney's wound, he pulled him upright and picked up his rifle. "Benjamin, you better talk. What were you doing here?"

Benjamin looked cowardly, his face pale in the moonlight, his voice trembling. "I saw something in the bushes when I was coming up from the stables and thought I'd follow. I found this criminal sneaking around. Not knowing what kind of crime he had planned, I ambushed him. There's a price on his head, Father. A bounty!"

"With what weapon were you going to use to catch a murderer, son?"

Benjamin pulled a large dagger from his belt and showed his father. Adele gasped, drawing attention to herself. Shock didn't overwhelm her because the dagger was a wicked-looking beast of

189

metal—though it was—but because of why they were here late at night. They were looking for Grai and meant to end his life. Adele had led them to him.

"Give me that," Uncle Nicholas demanded. Benjamin relinquished the dagger and Uncle Nicholas threw it atop another knife he had confiscated from Delaney.

"Benjamin, you and Adele sit over there on that bench." He hoisted Delaney to his feet.

"Delaney, what are you doing here on Cyrus Madison's property?"

"I'm not talking to anyone but a lawyer." The man said. Adele could see him well now. The drawing on the wanted poster had been an accurate likeness. Delaney had pitted skin and a dark mustache. His eyes were black, almost deathly looking, with dark bushy brows. He had a scar on his cheek and the same bandana he wore that afternoon tied around his neck.

"What do you know about this man, Adele?"

"Nothing. Except...except that he followed me home from town today. And he threatened me."

"You and I are due for a long talk," her uncle told her. "As soon as I come back from town, I want every last detail. I don't care whether it's in the middle of the night or not. Go to the house and don't come out again. Benjamin, you're coming with me."

"You want me to go to the marshals?" Benjamin's voice squeaked like a mouse. For having tried to murder someone, the man had no backbone.

"Help me get this man to the road."

With that her uncle hoisted Delaney under his arms, Benjamin supported Delaney's weight from the other side, and they dragged the convict down the trail.

"You'd better 'fess up," she heard Delaney whisper to Benjamin as Adele watched him limp away. She did nothing until they were out of sight and a hush returned to the night. Soon the sound of the horses' hooves and carriage wheels faded away as well. Adele picked up the gauze that had dropped. There was no way to clean away the soiled snow, and so she didn't try. Her hands trembled as she packed everything back into the medicine bag. Thoughts rushed through her mind. This was her fault. She had put Grai's life in jeopardy. She should never have gone into Port Summerhill. If she hadn't, no one would have heard her questions, nor seen her buy gauze, nor followed her home.

She turned to go and there in front of her stood Grai's spirit.

She had not been terrified the first time she saw the ghostly form, but tonight his presence sent a chill up her spine, and she stepped back. No lovely smile greeted her, only a cold, unforgiving glare met her eyes.

"Grai wants you to leave. To never return."

The words broke her heart, and she shook her head. Tears streamed down her cheeks. "Please don't send me away."

"Those were Grai's words."

"I am so sorry," she pleaded.

He turned and floated toward the root cellar, but before he disappeared completely, he rolled around and looked at her with those soft sympathetic eyes she'd seen the first day they met.

"I am sorry, as well, Adele."

Forsaken

Grai hadn't bothered to light a lantern, darkness had become his refuge. No longer did he feel a companion to goodness. How quickly his life had plummeted to the abyss! From a young man enjoying the struggle of pursuing education and success—holding onto hope and purpose, thinking that he would soon achieve his dreams, to this! Attacked, nearly killed, separated from his soul, tumbling through the night with no direction, only to reach out one last time to someone who vowed deliverance. A gentle hand, a soft smile, promising eyes, and a caring heart and then as if a branch snapped, she let him go. What had he left? Yes. Darkness was his friend.

He sat on the stone shelf, having pushed aside the blankets that Adele had given him. He wanted nothing to do with her any longer. Her betrayal cut him deeper than the dagger had. He could trust no one in this world. No one!

His spirit slid into the dugout, illuminated by its ridiculous glow, a pout on his face. Grai looked aside.

"I told her."

"Good," Grai said, wincing as he sat up. The wound still hurt and itched. He needed a clean wrap. If he had to, he could wash this one with water from the fountain and go without a covering. Perhaps letting air to it would be best.

"You'll regret chasing her away," his spirit leaned against the wall, his arms folded.

"I'll regret nothing."

"She said she was sorry."

"For what?" Grai asked, locking on to the spirit's eyes. "For bringing Delaney and her cousin here to stab me? Or for bringing her uncle here to shoot me? Which one?"

"I don't think she did either, purposefully."

"Either way, if she's foolish enough to allow louts to follow her, then she's too naïve for me to be around."

"But you love her."

"Love? Nonsense. She's a stranger. How could I love a stranger?"

"Don't do that, Grai. Don't deny your affection toward her."

Grai set his jaw, steeling against any emotion that attempted to slide into him from his spirit. "If I felt anything at all, it was because of you."

"Of course, it was."

"I don't need it. I'm fine hiding out until I heal."

"Which Adele has been helping you to do."

"If she helped with anything, she showed me who the conspirators are."

His spirit snickered. "You think you know who the conspirators are, but in actuality, you know nothing!"

"And your source of information is?"

"I have none."

"Exactly." Grai stood, eager to be out of such close quarters with the phantom.

"Are they gone?" Grai asked.

"Yes. All of them."

His spirit trailed him through the tunnel like a badgering old woman. Grai resented being told what he thought, what he felt, or what he should do. The spirit had no mind, no common sense, but prodded him with emotions he didn't care to have—that he'd be better off not having.

"What are you going to do, Grai?" his spirit asked.

"I'm going to think. I'm going to make a decision and try to keep your opinion out of it."

"A decision on what?"

"On whether I should drown you in the fountain."

"You can't do that."

"I can," Grai argued.

"You'll die. I'll live. It will give you no satisfaction."

"I'll take my chances."

Grai pushed on the stone that sealed the root cellar and stepped into the chill of the night. He breathed deeply, causing his wound to ache. Unbuttoning his coat, he threw it on the statue of his grandfather's dog, pulled his shirt over his head, and unwrapped the dressing. Adele had taken the medicine bag, and so he had no clean gauze and the fountain water had frozen. Icicles would work. He broke off the longest spike he could find on the wisteria and rubbed it over his lesion.

"Put your coat over your shoulders so you don't freeze to death," his spirit ordered.

That his spirit bade him to do anything aggravated Grai, but the frosty night air had become unbearable, and so he took the advice and pulled his coat over his shoulders. He sat on the bench, shivering while the ice numbed the gash. Once the spike had melted, Grai slipped into his shirt again and put his coat on. His teeth chattered, but he didn't want to go back into the root cellar. No matter the frost, the stars beckoned him to linger.

The universe understood his loneliness, his insignificance. He identified with the void. Huddled in his coat, his body trembling, he rose and began walking, and like a magnet, the trail under the hoarfrost drew him to the gate and the view of Barrington's manor.

"What are you hoping for, Grai?" his spirit whispered near to his ear. Grai felt the warmth of his energy and stepped away in fear of absorbing his spirit's kindness. Should he yield to honesty, his heart would break, and he feared he'd no longer have the will to live.

"Hope? I'm not sure there's anything left to hope for." Grai answered. No lights brightened the tower where he had once seen her. He supposed that was her bedchamber window, for more than once she had pulled the curtain open and looked his way. "I didn't want Adele to be involved. I told you it would be wrong."

"Has it really been that bad?"

Bad? He'd seen it all, everything that happened. Grai had been outside near his dugout when he heard the men coming for him. If he had wandered any farther into the courtyard, they would have tackled him. Being without a weapon, they would have killed him. Bad? According to whose principles? Bad that he might have been killed? Or bad that he had survived?

"You saw her cousin sneaking around in the woods with a dagger the size of a saber," Grai said.

"It wasn't that large," his spirit argued.

"How would he have known we were here?"

"He frequents the Barrington's house. He could have found us the same way Adele did."

"Or followed her. What makes you think she didn't lead him here on purpose?"

"Why would she?"

"And what about that other fellow, Delaney?"

"Delaney was an apprentice to your grandfather's partner. You know that! Delaney knew you before Adele did. And Delaney knows about the gold."

"They didn't attack me for gold the first time."

"No."

"You think Adele led them to you? I don't," his spirit said.

Grai turned to look at him. Could the two of them ever agree on anything?

"And why don't you?"

"She loves you."

Grai shook his head. He refused to believe it. "If she loved me, then why did these people suddenly show up tonight after she went to Port Summerhill? No one knew I was here before tonight."

"I have no answers for you, Grai. She may have turned on you, but my heart tells me she didn't."

"Your heart? It's my heart as well, you know!" Grai's tone made the spirit quiver. "This is the second woman who has turned on me. First my mother. Now Adele. Does that matter to you at all?"

"You distrust people before you know the facts. For that reason alone, you and I are disjointed. You can never love unless you trust."

"And I can never trust if I'm betrayed."

"You are correct."

Grai turned back toward the manor, satisfied he made his point.

"You are wrong in your judgment of people, however. Because of that, any hope for her affection is lost."

When the spirit drifted away from him, Grai shivered again. It didn't matter. His spirit felt no cold, Grai felt no love—in a sense, there was a harmony to that, each resolving a crisis in their own way.

The manor appeared so empty now, so hollow and deserted. Already regret churned Grai's stomach, and he wished he hadn't condemned her. He wanted to care for her. He wanted her near him. He wanted to be one with his spirit and feel for her, but he didn't have the strength to bear any more pain.

Nicholas' Fears

Adele cried herself to sleep.

Not because she had been orphaned, or shamed, or even that her uncle had threatened to commit her to an insane asylum— she had heard horror stories of what they were like. What brought her despondency to the surface was that she had fallen in love with a man who asked her to never return. She had failed him in every way possible, even though she tried so hard to save him. He had been a light in a dark tunnel for her. He had watched over her in her grief. He had loved her in his own extraordinary way. And now he wanted her gone.

In the morning when she woke, the same worries burdened her, and she trembled on her bed so much so that Butterscotch came to her and licked her salty tears. Adele caressed the cat and held her close until the feline's purring eased the pain in her heart.

"As much as I have reason to, I cannot lie here all morning feeling sorry for myself and counting my woes," she said to the cat. "I need to be of use. I'll ask Mei Ling to teach me to cook today then I could spend the rest of my life working in the kitchen. I'm not an aristocrat, Butterscotch. The Creator didn't form me from the same clay as Aunt Eloise and Uncle Nicholas. I'll never be noble, honorable, or impressive. I'm not even sure if I fit into the working class. I hope I'm not a criminal. Do you think Uncle Nicholas is right?" She scratched behind Butterscotch's ears. "Do you think I, too, will follow the footsteps of my parents?"

The only answer she got from the cat was a gentle purr. She sat up and dried her eyes with her hands.

"Silks and satins are for blue-blooded people, not I. Why did I assume I could save anyone?" She stroked Butterscotch's soft fur again. "I didn't want this to happen, but I think I love him!" Looking out the window from her bed, beyond the frosted glass and snowy yard to the dormant honeysuckle, she whispered. "I love him. I'm sure I do."

Adele chose a simple linen skirt and bodice that she had brought from Port Galleon, brushed her hair, and tied it in a braid.

"Come downstairs with me," she told Butterscotch. "Let's see what life will bring us now that we've ruined everything I could ever hope to have."

Butterscotch scurried past Adele when she opened the door and trotted down the stairs with an odd crook in her tail that prompted a smile through her tears.

Sunlight filtered into the house from the window in the foyer, and more so in the living room. What snow blanketed the ground outside glimmered so brilliantly Adele had to squint and drop the drapes before she could open her eyes fully. Uncle Nicholas and Aunt Eloise were on the couch. Neither acknowledged her when she first descended the stairs. Uncle Nicholas leaned over with his head buried in his hands, and Aunt Eloise gently stroked his back, comforting him. Auntie looked up at her with a frown after Adele closed the drapes.

"Please, your uncle is not feeling well. Let us alone," she said softly.

"No!" Uncle Nicholas argued with an unfamiliar passion. "We should talk, Adele."

Adele stood in front of them, wringing her hands. She had already experienced more turmoil than her nerves could manage. Anymore

198

would surely cause her to go daft.

"Sit down," he said.

Adele took a chair across from them and Aunt Eloise leaned back, a hankie in her hands.

Her uncle sat upright, his hair askew, his eyes red. He looked as though he hadn't any sleep and judging by his clothes he wore the night before, he might have recently come back from Port Summerhill. Adele assumed his distress came from shooting a man. Or perhaps because Delaney gave him trouble on the way to the marshal's office. Aunt Eloise scooted away from him and picked up her knitting from a basket at the end of the couch, a gesture meant to put Adele at ease. Nothing could put her at ease.

"I need to know the truth, Adele. Everything."

Adele shrugged, not knowing where to begin.

"How often did you speak with Delaney? How close were you to him? When did your conspiring begin?"

Adele took a deep breath. "I never conspired with him. I only spoke with him once, and then I didn't know who he was. He had his face covered."

Uncle Nicholas raised his chin, crossed his arms, and leaned back.

"I rode to Port Summerhill yesterday, and he followed me home. And threatened me!"

Her uncle held up his hand and shook his head. "Wait! You took my horse into Port Summerhill?"

"Yes, sir."

"Well, at least you're honest about that! I already had full knowledge. Mr. Fernsworth told me you borrowed a horse and asked for directions into town. I could have forgiven such an act for a young lady wanting to ride. I would never have consented to your riding into Port Summerhill alone in a snowstorm. That was foolish."

It was, but not for the reasons Uncle Nicholas thought. Adele cleared her throat.

"Tell me why you went."

Adele's hands sweated. She could not tell her story without mentioning Grai. Then again, Grai had already rebuked her. She had no more promises to keep, although her love for him remained, and always would. After last night, the way her uncle handled Delaney, and even Benjamin, the chances of Uncle Nicholas being a suspect had diminished. She risked nothing telling her aunt and uncle the truth.

"Before you begin," Uncle Nicholas interrupted her thoughts. "I am aware that someone or something is living on the Madison's property. Last night I had a very disturbing experience."

Adele bit her lip.

"Some sort of apparition came out of the ivy, large and ghastly. It had the face of a man, but the rest of its body was transparent and flew like a cloud of dust. It terrified me. The first shot I fired hit it, or rather went through it."

Adele gasped. "What happened to it?"

"It fled."

Adele went cold. No wonder Grai's spirit had been so grisly to her. What horror that must have been for Grai! It wasn't bad enough that the thugs had come back to murder him, but her uncle came shooting at his spirit. Grai must think she sent them all.

"Have you seen this thing?"

Adele nodded.

"What is it?"

Her hands quivered so violently that she held them down on her lap. "I'm afraid to tell you."

"Why?"

"Because you might…" The words wouldn't come, but the tears were struggling to find their way out. "You mustn't…Please don't shoot him again! Please don't kill him."

Her uncle's lips grew thin, and he squinted at her. "Who? What are you talking about?"

"The ghost is not a dead man. He's only a severed spirit."

"Severed from what?"

Adele shuddered and glanced at Aunt Eloise, who had stopped her knitting.

"From Grai Madison."

Her aunt set her knitting on her lap and Uncle Nicholas sat quiet, like a statue.

"Grai Madison is alive?" Aunt Eloise asked.

"Please don't kill him. He's a beautiful person. His spirit is kind and gentle. Something happened to him. Men attacked him and they wounded him terribly. I took your medicine bag to nurse his wounds."

Uncle Nicholas and Aunt Eloise locked eyes.

"He didn't want me to tell anyone because he thinks whoever tried to kill him will try again. He's hiding until he and his spirit…," she covered her face. "It's such a horrid predicament."

"That poor boy! He's living there by himself in the cold?" Aunt Eloise asked.

"There's a root cellar he stays in."

"How much do you know about him? Did you see this cellar where he stays?" Aunt Eloise asked.

"I know of the root cellar," Uncle Nicholas interrupted. "It's been said there is a cache of gold that Cyrus Madison hid away on his property. Coins he and the professor collected during the war. This might explain why Delaney was snooping around the area. But it doesn't explain Adele's involvement. Nor does it explain this…this ghost!"

"It's not just the gold that Delaney wants, Uncle. It's Grai. They tried to kill Grai once," Adele added. "Or at least someone did. Grai thinks his stepfather hired ruffians to murder him so that Bonneville

201

would inherit the property."

"That's preposterous!" Uncle Nicholas sprang from the couch. "Bonneville is cunning, and crafty, yes, but he would never harm either of his sons."

"He has more than one?"

"Nicholas," Aunt Eloise warned. "We're not to speak of Matt."

"Matt? Matt is Bonneville's son?"

"Illegitimate," Nicholas added. "The world isn't supposed to know about Mary Sellers and Richard Bonneville's illegitimate affair. Even though it occurred long before Grai's mother married him, he had kept it a secret from her. The ordeal, when she found out, is what made Lucille go barmy. Eloise said you danced with Matt?"

"Once. He wanted to dance more, but I refused him." Adele's heart raced, and though she listened in on the conversation, her mind spun.

"Regardless of his personal life, Bonneville is a lot of things, a rogue yes, but he's not a killer. So, you've told me about young Mr. Madison and his estate, now tell me what you were doing in Port Summerhill?"

"Grai wanted to stop probate somehow until he could discover who his assailants were. He has a Will but is certain whoever tried to kill him would finish the job if he showed himself. I suggested letting me help to find a lawyer. Grai planned on coming out of hiding as soon as…" she looked at her auntie. This sounded so eldritch. "As soon as his ghost and he were one again. I guess I made a fatal mistake going to speak with Mary Sellers." She rose. "Delaney somehow knew of my inquiries and that Grai was still alive. He saw me in the mercantile when I purchased the gauze. I think he assumed I was going to use it to nurture Grai's wounds. He followed me to the junction and then threatened me."

Aunt Eloise put her hand over her mouth. "Oh, Adele!"

"What did he say when he threatened you?"

"He wanted to know where Grai was. I refused to acknowledge that I knew who he was talking about, but I guess I don't make a particularly good liar. That he and Benjamin were on the property armed tells me they were going to finish what they had started."

"Now you're accusing Benjamin of attempted murder?" Uncle Nicholas asked, his chest puffed, his face red and his fists clenched.

Adele shrugged. "Why else was he there?"

Uncle Nicholas spun around and walked to the window. Adele looked at her aunt.

"Benjamin is not a killer either," Aunt Eloise insisted.

"We don't know that Eloise," her uncle claimed.

"Is there any other reason you would suspect Benjamin was involved?" Aunt Eloise asked Adele with pleading eyes. As much as Adele wanted to satisfy her aunt's fears, she had to be honest.

"Peter has Grai's timepiece. Grai's grandfather gave it to him. It has Cyrus Madison's initials on it. I'm sure it's his."

Aunt Eloise leaned back, her face pale. "Oh dear," she whispered. After a moment of fanning herself, she added. "Perhaps he found the watch. Or perhaps Benjamin purchased it from somewhere."

"Perhaps," Adele agreed, not wanting to upset her aunt. Aunt Eloise lost her sister to crime. How horrid would it be to lose a son as well? "I'm sure we can sort this out."

"Why would Benjamin or Delaney kill Grai Madison?" Uncle Nicholas growled. "Neither one of them would get anything for it but a noose around their necks. Delaney is already sentenced to hang. He was after the gold, that's all. And Benjamin was trying to get the bounty money on Delaney's head. I have no reason not to believe him. This idea of a conspiracy is far-fetched, Adele."

"If that's what you believe."

Adele stood, anticipating being excused. Mei Ling had come into the kitchen through the back door, getting ready to prepare the morning meal. This would be a good day to learn to cook.

"I think with Delaney in jail, we've done our duty. There needn't be any more conversation concerning the matter."

"And Grai?"

"Grai can rest assured the thief has been apprehended."

Adele looked anxiously at her aunt and then at her uncle. "That's all you're going to do about the matter?"

"I do not need to do anything else. You, though, must answer for the necklace." He glanced at the foyer, at the sound of a carriage. "And speak of the angels, my daughter has just arrived. Your time to exonerate yourself is at hand."

Lila and her children walked inside at that very moment. Lila, hearing her father's words, quickly removed her coat and boots, and stormed into the living room.

"Am I late for this conversation, Father?"

"On the contrary, you're just in time."

Lila blustered in front of Adele, her green and red plaid skirt flaming in the sunlight that still trickled in from the partially covered window. Lila's blond hair had been braided in one long braid that fell to her waist. Her skin was flushed from the cold weather, which made her look alive and livid. Her blue eyes shone like topaz under her blond lashes.

"What do you have to say for yourself, before I go to Port Summerhill to speak with Marshal Carrey today?"

Maggie hurried into the living room and interrupted Butterscotch's nap by sitting on the floor and pulling her onto her lap. Peter strolled to the hearth and stood by the fire. He had a strange look on his face, almost fearful. Adele merely glimpsed at him, noticing he took an extreme interest in his mother's words.

"I didn't steal your necklace."

"You're a liar, Adele."

"I'm not."

"What was it doing in your room then?"

"I have no idea. I didn't put it there." She looked at Peter again, whose eyes grew wide. The second that Adele let down her guard, a sharp pain stung her cheek.

"Mama, don't!" Peter cried.

"Lila!" Aunt Eloise jumped from the couch, but she was not in time to stop Lila from slapping Adele again.

When Lila pulled back her arm to strike a third time, Adele grabbed her hand and stopped her.

"Mama, don't!" Maggie jumped up screaming, the cat hid under the couch.

Adele gritted her teeth, wrestling against Lila's strength, the two pushing each other about the room.

Rage had been swelling inside Adele—for being everyone's scapegoat, for being suspected of crimes she didn't do, for being slandered and degraded. She wanted to sock her cousin in the eye, make it black and blue, spoil that pretty face of hers, but she restrained herself, satisfied with just keeping Lila's strikes at bay.

"You're a liar and a thief." Lila spat. "You aren't good enough to live with my mother and father. I think you deserve to be hanged just like your parents were, what with all the trouble you brought. You're going to prison, Adele."

The powerful arms of her uncle pulled Adele away from Lila, and Aunt Eloise took Lila by the shoulders.

"I've not done any of those things!" Adele roared.

"Stop, Lila!" Aunt Eloise commanded.

"Stop!" Peter echoed. He squeezed in front of his mother. His high-pitched voice drowned Lila's accusations and his grandmother's pleas.

"Don't Mama. Don't let them hang Adele. I took the necklace

and put it in the tower. It's my fault. I wanted her gone, but not dead. Stop!"

Lila squirmed away from her mother's hold and stepped back. Gasping for breath, she glared open-mouth at her son. Uncle Nicholas released Adele, and Aunt Eloise picked Maggie up in her arms after the child came running to her.

"What did you say?" Lila asked.

Tears ran down Peter's cheeks. "I didn't mean to put her in jail. I just wanted her gone after what she did to Uncle Ben. Not dead though."

"What did she do to Uncle Ben?" Uncle Nicholas asked.

"She kicked him."

All eyes were on Adele, but Adele didn't say a word. She wasn't about to defend herself again. No one believed anything she said before, why would they now?

Lila straightened her skirt and after glancing at her parents, she took Peter by the hand and guided him to the couch where she sat with him and the two conversed quietly.

Uncle Nicholas, clearly beside himself, paced, shooting angry looks at both Adele and Eloise.

Peter continued to cry and rub his eyes.

The conversation with the boy ended shortly, and Lila rose.

"Well, Mother, Father, I am sorry for this outrage in your home. Please forgive me." She waited for an answer. Aunt Eloise nodded. Uncle Nicholas seemed in shock.

An odd silence followed.

"Adele, I was mistaken about the necklace. My apologies."

Adele's cheeks flamed with pain where Lila had slapped her, and she wondered if they now glowed as red as Lila's. She said nothing. The apology was only for the accusation about the necklace, nothing more. Adele turned and ran up the stairwell to her room. She had no desire to talk to anyone after that display. She shut her door, stormed across the room, pulled back her curtains, opened her window, and screamed.

"Grai!"

He wouldn't answer. She didn't want him to. He hated her. She'd never see him again. It didn't matter. His name meant life to her, and she cried out again, and then she slammed the window shut. If Uncle Nicholas meant what he said about committing her to an asylum, now he had a good excuse.

She fell on the bed, folded her arms, and resisted crying. She'd run away. Perhaps she'd return to Port Galleon and become a woman of the night, tease men, and steal their money. Why not? She already had a reputation without ever having done anything. What would hold her back?

A knock on her door interrupted her plans.

Aunt Eloise stepped inside, and Adele leaped from the bed.

"Adele, we're so sorry."

"Whatever you're going to tell me now has no bearing on what was said before. Neither can your words wash away what I know Uncle Nicholas and Lila and Peter and Benjamin think of me. You're the only one who has given me any kindness and I thank you. But the rest of the family wants me gone and I'm ready to pack my bags."

"No, Adele. Don't. Listen to me for a moment."

Adele's cheeks flushed. Tired of listening. What could Aunt Eloise say that would soothe her soul?

"You began something that I think you should finish."

"What did I begin?"

"You took it upon yourself to be a nurse for Grai Madison. You can't desert him. He needs you to follow up on what you've begun."

Adele gaped at her aunt.

"Don't just stand there gawking at me. The poor man is suffering. I would feel as responsible as you if he should die. He's a fine young man. An architect, isn't he?" Aunt Eloise asked.

"He's already drawn blueprints of the manor he's going to build," Adele admitted.

"Take care of him," Aunt Eloise whispered. "You must help him get well."

"I have your permission?" Adele looked out the window again. Nothing stirred save for water dripping from the icicles on the eaves making perfectly round cavities in the snow below.

"You have my instruction. I'm not sure why one's spirit would be severed from a body. Perhaps a priest could help."

"I think he just needs a gentle touch," Adele admitted.

"You talk as if you've already given him a gentle touch."

Adele sat on the bed, picked up her pillow, and held it close to her chest. "I have fallen in love with him, both his spirit and Grai himself. I want to see him better and safe and those who are conspiring against him locked away. He blames the railroad, Auntie. Because his grandfather's property is targeted as grounds for a terminal, he thinks someone has conspired against him."

"I suppose that's possible, although he could offer to sell and be done with all of this kerfuffle."

"He won't sell. He loves his grandfather's estate too much."

"Still, it seems there would be a way to negotiate for a part of the property for the railroad?"

"He's not in a position to talk to anyone at the moment."

With a long sigh and a tender expression, Aunt Eloise sat next to Adele and stroked her hair. "You've been through so much. I'm terribly sorry for the additional turmoil your uncle and I have put you through."

"I need to go back to Port Summerhill."

Aunt Eloise's eyes popped open. "Whatever for?"

"I have unfinished business there."

Her aunt rose and walked to the window, staring out across the garden to the Madison's property. She sighed, shaking her head. "Very well. You've gotten yourself in this deep, I suppose you should finish what you started. Have Fernsworth drive the buggy this time. Tell him I told him to bring a rifle and follow you wherever you go. Be home before dark." She smiled and tapped Adele on the nose. "Don't talk to strangers."

"What about Uncle Nicholas?"

"I've already taken care of your uncle. He won't bother you."

Uncovered

A dele inhaled the freshness of the morning and welcomed the sensation of new life the frosty air brought. She hadn't ever been so confident, and to her, Port Summerhill hadn't looked so colorful. With the weather warming, snow melted leaving muddy streets and piles of crusty ice that bordered the wooden boardwalk. Sunlight shimmered in puddles on the road, and steam drifted off rooftops.

After having stopped at the jailhouse, Mr. Fernsworth reined in the mules in front of the bank, jumped to the ground, and opened her door. Adele took his hand as support and stepped down.

"Careful of the mud, Miss Adele," he said.

She gave him a smile and squeezed his hand.

"I'm becoming much more aware of murky things these days, thank you, Mr. Fernsworth. Wait for me I won't be but a few minutes."

"Yes ma'am."

She breathed the frosty air and soaked in a moment of sunshine. The day could not be brighter, she thought to herself, for today she would win her prize. No one could stop her now!

She wore a dress she borrowed from her auntie this morning, no more of the poor girl's woollies, and lifted her skirt so that mud wouldn't soil it. Once on the boardwalk, she adjusted the scarf that tied her hat, took a deep breath, and smiled again at Mr. Fernsworth. He nodded in return. When she eyed Marshal Carry stepping into the street with two deputies walking toward her, she opened the door.

Only a few people were in the bank, mostly tellers and two financiers holding a private conversation by the windows along the wall. Adele skipped the formalities and walked down the hall daring anyone to stop her, her head held high, the shine of her skirt catching sun rays that filtered through the eyebrow windows above her.

She raised her hand to knock on Mary Seller's door, reconsidered, turned the brass handle, and walked in uninvited. The woman she sought stood and her son, the red-headed Matt, jumped from his seat in surprise.

"What is this?" Miss Sellers asked.

"This is the person who has discovered your corruption, Miss Sellers, and I want you to know you haven't, nor will you ever get away with your lethal scheme to make your son rich."

"What are you talking about?" Mary asked and turned to Matt. "Go summons the marshal."

Matt brushed by Adele on his way out the door.

"You needn't go far, he's on his way here, already," Adele responded.

He stopped and turned.

"I want you to know before you're arrested, Miss Sellers, that you near ruined the life of the kindest, most gentle man in all of Port Summerhill. I want you to know that what you did to him scared him horrendously, and it could have been for life, but it won't be. He'll rise above your nasty ruse and live to be a great man. Everyone who knows him will love him. Not so with you, Miss Sellers. Your evil plot to ruin him has turned on you."

The door opened, and Adele stepped back as Marshal Carry entered with his deputies.

"Sorry for this intrusion, Miss Sellers, but I'm going to have to arrest you for attempted murder."

"That's absurd. I did nothing." She paled and held her hand over her heart. "You can't arrest me on the word of this…this street woman!"

"Miss Adele brought our attention to the matter, and we have a confession from one of our prisoners. If it hadn't been for Adele here, we wouldn't have thought to ask."

"What prisoner? Who would say such a thing?"

"Benjamin Barrington, ma'am. One of your hitmen."

The deputies each took one of her arms.

"Wait! Stop," she protested. Her hat fell off her head as she struggled. "I never meant for them to kill him. I only wanted them to take his briefcase."

The deputies lessened their hold on her. She straightened her dress and fixed her hat. "I didn't ask them to hurt him. I was only after documents concerning the estate. I'm not responsible for what they did to him. We wanted the Will, that's all."

"For what, Miss Sellers?" Adele asked.

Tears formed in the woman's eyes. "To destroy it, what else? If there were no Will, then Richard would have the deed, and he promised when the property sold Matt would have a share of the profits. It's the least he could do for us. I was only looking out for my son's benefit."

"And who looked out for Grai's?" Adele asked.

"Miss Sellers, you can plead your case in court. If you don't come willingly now, we must be rough with you. Is that what you want?"

"Mother let them take you, we'll fight it in court," Matt said. "And we'll see to it you won't bother us again," he told Adele.

"Don't be threatening Miss Adele," Marshal Carry interrupted him. "If anything happens to her, we'll know who to come for."

The deputies bound Miss Sellers and escorted her out the door. Her son, red faced, followed.

Adele waited a moment in the office, eyeing the papers on Mary

Seller's desk—probate papers with Bonneville's signature. Next to them, soaking on an ink pad, was a notary stamp. Adele took the papers, folded them carefully and tucked them in her purse.

.

The Estate

Adele didn't go inside the house after Mr. Fernsworth helped her out of the carriage at her uncle's doorstop and drove off. Instead, she took the pathway to the garden enjoying the warmth of the sun's winter rays,

Damp brown leaves dropped in clusters when Adele opened the gate under the honeysuckle. She brushed them off her shawl, held her silk skirt ankle-high over her boots with one hand, her hat with her other hand, and ducked under the pale branches. When she reached the patio, she swept leaves from her clothing and plucked twigs from the veil of her bonnet.

Water trickled from the fountain in the courtyard, melting the thin sheets of ice as it flowed through. Sunlight cast soft, blue shadows across the marble statue's features. Across from the fountain, on the bench, Adele had so often occupied, sat Grai—the man—a pad of paper on his lap and a pencil and straightedge in his hand. He hadn't seen her. Too focused on his drafting, he studied the ruined columns that once held the entry to his grandfather's manor, and drew another line, counting and measuring.

Grai's spirit appeared from behind him and stared at her. He opened his mouth to speak, but closed it again, instead nudging Grai and disappearing into him, causing Adele double vision when she looked at Grai.

Grai glanced at her.

When their eyes adhered to each other, Adele's body tingled. She wanted to run to him, embrace him, but she stood her ground, cautious. He said nothing.

"Mary Sellers was just arrested," Adele stated.

Grai set his work to the side.

"She had hired Delaney and Benjamin as assassins to take your life so that her son, Matt, your step-father's illegitimate child, would inherit your grandfather's estate. I walked in on them just as she was about to notarize the paperwork."

Grai stood.

Such a handsome man with his curls glistening in the sunlight. He must have washed his shirt, it sparkled so.

"Matt is Bonneville's son? I thought Mary was a widow...,"

Adele shook her head. "He kept his secret well. Until now."

She pulled the paperwork from her purse and held it out to him.

"You're safe now, Grai. I just thought you'd want to know."

His silence bothered her. She had no idea what he was thinking and her heartbeat so hard her instincts told her to run, but she didn't. He stepped up to her and took the paperwork out of her hands. His spirit quivered in and out of him, and she could see the struggle he was going through fighting him. He glanced briefly at the paperwork, folded it, and tucked it into his shirt pocket.

"Thank you."

"It was the least I could do, after bungling so badly in town the other day. If I had known Mary Sellers was involved, I never would have gone to her. I'm sure she had Matt order Delaney to follow me. I'm so sorry that happened."

"Your uncle...,"

"Your silly spirit scared my uncle out of his wits," she laughed. "Shooting your ghost was merely a reaction to terror."

"He knows, now."

"He knows Grai Madison is alive. Yes. He doesn't admit that what he shot was a ghost. He thinks he went daft for a moment because of his rage. But he knows Benjamin was one of the men who tried to kill you."

Grai closed his eyes, and when he did, the double vision ceased. Adele looked around the courtyard for his spirit, but she didn't see him.

"You are the most beautiful woman in the world, Adele," he whispered with his eyes still closed. His face turned red and when he opened his eyes again, tears swelled at their corners. He took her hands, cupped them together, and brought them to his lips. With a warm breath, he kissed them.

"Forgive me," he said.

"Forgive you for what?"

"For fighting against my love for you. I've accepted it now."

His words robbed her of her breath. Of all the things she had expected, it was not a confession of his love for her.

"Grai, I…," she stuttered.

"You've proven your love more than once. Even when you walked away in tears, thinking I never wanted to see you again, you continued to fight for me. I'm overwhelmed, Adele." His entire body shook. At first, Adele thought his wound had gotten worse, and that maybe he had an infection.

"Grai, are you well?"

"Hold me," he said.

Adele pulled off her hat and dropped it to the ground. She slipped her arms around his waist, careful not to rub against his wound, and held him tightly. His body grew hot, and the shaking increased, so she held him tighter. He grasped her as if his life depended on her touch.

"Good heavens, it's happening," he said.

"What Grai?"

216

Her stillness finally soothed his trembling. He breathed a sigh of relief, kissed her hair gently, and then relaxed.

"I think I'm healed," he whispered.

"You and your spirit have become one again?"

"I think so. Saying I love you isn't enough, though. I want to marry you, to live with you forever. I will rebuild my grandfather's estate for us to live in, to raise a family in."

She held him tighter. She would never let him go, no matter what happened.

Epilogue

Adele stood by the storm porch door, her hands folded across her chest, watching Grai and the children in the garden. Grai played chase with them in his woolen frock, his curls tucked under a top hat that Uncle Nicholas had given him.

"Breakfast is ready," she finally called after Mei Ling scolded her for keeping the door open. She adored seeing Grai with the children. Peter had taken to following Grai around as he once had with Benjamin. He clung to Grai's arm as tightly as Maggie did as the three of them came to the house.

Aunt Eloise had given Grai a guest room and insisted the doctor make regular visits. It took two weeks before the wound closed up. The doctor warned that he was on the verge of infection and if he hadn't come into the Barrington household when he did, he may very well have died. During his convalescence, Grai had been a comfort for Peter when the boy found out that his uncle Benjamin wouldn't be returning for a while. When Peter returned the timepiece to Grai, they bonded and had become inseparable.

Adele shut the door behind them and helped arrange the croissants on the tray.

"You baked these?" Grai asked.

"I did. Mei Ling is an excellent teacher."

He tried to snatch one off the tray, but she slapped his hand. This was the first formal meal she had prepared for the family after training with Mei Ling. The servant was in high spirits.

"She's good, no? Best help in the kitchen. Now go, sit down. I will serve."

With Thanksgiving only a week away, the family's cornucopia already adorned the table with squash, colored corn, and apples from neighboring farms. Autumn colors tinted the décor, and Aunt Eloise had hung her holiday curtains on the windows.

The children ran through the kitchen, laughing.

"Wash up!" Adele told them. Lila met Peter and Maggie in the living room, her cameo necklace hung delicately around her neck.

When Adele felt his arms wrapping around her from behind and blew in her ear, she giggled.

"Stop that," she said and pushed away from him. "Go sit at the table as Mei Ling told you to do." She put the tray of croissants in his hands and dodged away just as Aunt Eloise emerged from the hall.

Aunt Eloise wore one of her better tea dresses, off-white with delicate layers of lace and crêpe. Her hair done up in a soft bun, you'd think she hadn't seen her husband for a month even though it had only been three days. She peeked out into the foyer at the sound of a carriage.

"They're here!" she said.

All but Eloise stood behind their chairs at the table when the men walked in. Uncle Nicholas had barely put his hat on the rack and removed his coat when Auntie embraced him. Smiles turned to frowns as the two wayfarers entered the room. Neither Uncle Nicholas nor Bonneville shared the joy of their return.

"You must be famished," Aunt Eloise said.

Uncle Nicholas merely nodded and escorted Bonneville into the dining hall. When the man saw his stepson for the first time since the attack, he stopped in his tracks. Grai shivered, and for a moment when Adele caught him shaking, she swore she saw double. His face turned red and his cheeks swelled.

"Bonneville," Grai nodded slightly.

"They told me you were alive. I should have come sooner, but we were involved in…"

"No need to apologize. I wouldn't expect you to interrupt your business. The railroad is more important. I'm glad you got the letter about the Will and that all worked out smoothly. My apologies for not providing Port Summerhill with a Rail Depot. I trust there will be property elsewhere for that?" Grai swallowed and Adele took his hand, which he received eagerly. His shoulders relaxed when she touched him.

"Yes, the estate is taken care of. Congratulations. The land is yours."

The silence that followed lacked the friendliness a homecoming should have had. Aunt Eloise laughed with a nervous edge. "Please Nicholas, Richard, be seated. Adele has prepared a wonderful meal for us."

Uncle Nicholas looked at Adele and nodded. "I'm looking forward to it. I trust your lessons with Mei Ling have been going well."

"I enjoy cooking," Adele admitted.

The men stood by their chairs and Gareth, despite his usual quiet self, offered to say grace after which everyone took a seat and Mei Ling served. Adele glanced at Grai several times, but he focused on the food, scooping eggs onto his plate, and passing the tray to her. He purposefully avoided looking at his stepfather.

Aunt Eloise broke the silence.

"You had a safe and prosperous trip, I can assume?" she asked.

"Safe, yes," Uncle Nicholas spoke softly. He set his fork down and cleared his throat.

"I see no reason for not coming out with it. There is no railroad coming to Port Summerhill."

Adele gasped.

"None?" she asked.

"I'm afraid they gave the bid to territory south of here."

"Was it because of my failure to…," Grai began?

"No," Uncle Nicholas assured him. "It was not because of anything anyone here had done."

"After all that work, all those meetings and the reception. Why? What happened?" Aunt Eloise asked.

"The railroad council considered our proposal, but preferred Tacoma's location."

"It appears we have a mountain in the way," Bonneville interjected. "It never would have worked, anyway. Port Summerhill will have to find their fortune through other means."

Aunt Eloise reached out to Uncle Nicholas and squeezed his hand. "I'm sorry," she whispered.

After a moment of awkward silence as the family consumed their dinner, Grai tossed his napkin on the table and stood. His gesture surprised everyone.

"In lieu of this disappointing news, I would like a moment to thank you, Mr., and Mrs. Barrington, for your kindness and hospitality. I believe you both saved my life, and I am deeply grateful." Uncle Nicholas nodded, sitting back in his chair.

"Oh, Grai, we only did what any reasonable person would do when they see someone suffering," Aunt Eloise said.

"Mr. Barrington," Grai locked eyes with Uncle Nicholas. "I am uncertain how these things work. I mean, since Adele's parents are no longer with us, and since you are her legal guardian, I am assuming you would be the one to approach in this matter."

"What is it, son?" Uncle Nicholas asked.

"And I'm not sure if I should ask at the table or in private."

"Finish what you've begun."

"I would be deeply honored…" his voice tapered, and he choked on his words. "I would be more than honored. I would be elated if you would allow me Adele's hand in marriage."

Adele clasped her hands over her mouth as Grai waited for an answer.

Lila let out a cheer. Gareth smiled at Adele, the first time he had ever acknowledged her existence.

"Oh, my word, Grai!" Aunt Eloise exclaimed and stopped herself from saying more. A dutiful wife would wait for her husband's response.

Uncle Nicholas rose. Adele held her breath as he pushed his chair back and slowly moved away from his place at the head of the table. She thought he was going to leave the room and her heart stopped for a horrid moment. It didn't matter what he said, though. She would run away with Grai if she had to.

But Uncle Nicholas didn't walk away. Instead, he approached Grai and held out his hand.

"And I would be honored to have you in the family Grai Madison. And since there will be no railroad, I can spend my time helping you rebuild your grandfather's estate." They shook hands, and he patted Grai on the shoulder.

"We'll use my influence to get you some deals on building supplies. Stand up, young lady," he said to Adele. When she stood, he hugged her. Uncle Nicholas hugged her! She laughed, tears rolled down her cheeks.

"This pleases me," Uncle Nicholas admitted. "Yes. This pleases me." He slapped Grai on the arm again, pulled his pipe from his waistcoat pocket, and nodded to Bonneville. "Care to join me in the parlor?"

Bonneville's nod to Grai was cordial if that. He followed Uncle Nicholas.

"Well!" Aunt Eloise popped up from her chair. "I guess we'll be shopping for fabric soon!"

"Include me in this," Lila said. "Let me make the veil!"

The only people left at the table after that were Peter and Maggie, oblivious to everything else going on.

"Care to go for a little stroll?" Grai asked.

He took Adele's hand and led her to the foyer, helped her put on her coat, and then slipped into his. They stepped outside and Grai stopped at one of the garden beds, and to Adele's surprised, he touched a cold and wilted rosebud. When he did, a deep red blossom appeared.

"You will not diverge from who you are, will you?"

He laughed with that boyish grin she first fell in love with as his spirit. "Through and through," he said. He led her to the gate and touched the frost-covered honeysuckle that hung over them. Yellow flowers opened over the entire vine and as they bloomed a sweet fragrance perfumed the air. He pulled her close to him and as she nestled in the warmth of his arms, their lips met. She finally found a place where she belonged.

The End.

Notes on Historical Content

IN 1879 in a Pacific Northwest town, there was an attempted murder, a romance … and a ghost.

The Hoarfrost Mysteries are fictional stories created from a colorful era in American history.

Our fictional town Port Summerhill, is fashioned after the quaint seaport town of Port Townsend, WA, along the Puget Sound and Salish Sea. The date is 1879, when Washington was still a territory and the home to the S'Klallam tribe, pioneers, cavalry sent to protect the pioneers, businessmen with high ambitions, Chinese, and former southern slaves looking for a better life. A town whose history that is both colorful and dangerous, with tones of the Wild West. The S'Klallam tribe was the first to call Port Townsend home, then came the Europeans in 1851, and by the late 1800s, when our story begins in 1879, it boomed as a seaport with unrealized potential.

Today you'll find lovely Victorian homes, hotels, and establishments that mirror Port Townsend's history. The earliest buildings were constructed entirely of wood, but as the town prospered in the 1880s the homes were often replaced with "fireproof" brick structures. This historical data comes into play both in book one when Nicholas Barrington built his hotel and in book two, *Night Ice* when the bid for bricks became competitive.

The repeating theme of ghosts and spirits in the series is inspired by the many stories you'll find when visiting Port Townsend. Barrington's hotel, a facsimile of Manresa Castle, sports its own ghost or two and some of the other ghost legends of the area I plan on incorporating in future sequels of this fun mystery series.

As the Chinese servant of the Barringtons, Mei Ling embodies the early Chinese population in the Pacific Northwest. In the 1800s, Port Townsend served as a key immigration point and hub for a thriving Chinese community, including laborers and merchants, though the population fluctuated significantly due to discriminatory policies like the Chinese Exclusion Act. The Chinese established businesses, farms, and a community on the waterfront, with the Zee Tai Company being a notable and successful mercantile. The Chinese came by way of boat from British Columbia and often found passage with merchants who hired them as servants. Hostility showed its face, though, if border patrol boats intercepted them and often the Chinese were thrown overboard to avoid arrests, left to swim to shore, or drown.

It should be noted here that the Chinese had a heavy hand in building the railroad in the west and were prospective workers to continue the track to Port Townsend. In our story, Nicholas Barrington seeks to build that railroad, although the tracks never made it over the mountain and instead the railroad found its home in Tacoma.

Even though wood homes in Port Townsend were replaced by brick, fire continued to be a threat. However, *in the fall of 1885 a fire began at a blacksmith shop in the block between Taylor and Tyler streets,* destroying around 20 buildings. This is the backdrop for the opening scene in book three, **Wind in the Wilds**. *https://www.pthistory. com/fire/*

Hoarfrost to Roses, captures some of the customs and people known worldwide in the Victorian age. For instance, concerning the bodice that Adele's aunt purchases for her, the style is inspired by Princess Alexandra of Denmark (later Queen Alexandra) who was a fashion leader in the late 1800s, known for popularizing the "princess line" and cuirass bodices that created a new, form-fitting silhouette. https://fashionhistory.fitnyc.edu/1870-1879/

More interesting customs of the Victorian age that show up in book one include taking post-mortem images of children, tinplates that Adele notices on her auntie's mantel. Another interesting custom was the use of "hair rats" to lift a woman's hair into the desired height; these supports were made from their own hair that shed when brushed.

Grai's mother is extremely superstitious, and some of her fetishes include keeping a lock of Grai's hair in her locket when she believes him dead, which upsets Adele greatly.

Hoarfrost to Roses mentions other Victorian superstitions around death, such as covering mirrors after someone dies, so their spirit isn't trapped. And if you are the first to look in the mirror after a death, you will be the next one to die. Or to stop all clocks in the house at the exact moment of a death, believing it would help the soul transition. With varied symbolism, the act stood for time stopping for the deceased, the beginning of mourning, a way to avoid bad luck, and the prevention of the spirit's haunting of the home and its inhabitants. https://crystalcaudill.com/tbt-victorian-death-superstitions/

And of course, the tradition that a woman wore black during a period of mourning sometimes for up to a year after their loved one passed. It's little wonder we see so many images of women in those days wearing black, for with the high fatality rate, it seems a woman might mourn continually.

Out west, though, many of those traditions were lost, and so it was with Eloise Barrington who proves to be a progressive-minded woman, and her influence on Adele encourages the same. That she is breaking tradition creates animosity between her and Grai's mother. But

Eloise is of her own mind. This is seen in the next book **Night Ice** as she leads Adele into the women's suffrage movement.

A key figure is mentioned in **Night Ice**. The woman's name is Emily Olney, and she was the first woman to cast a ballot in the territory of Washington. Indeed, in 1883 (I revised the date to 1880 for story purposes) Washington made history by becoming one of the first places in the world to grant women the right to vote. However, the situation was not permanent. The vote was stolen from Washington women, a bitter pill to swallow. Indeed, it was repeatedly taken and then re-appropriated. It wasn't until Washington women took their fight beyond the legislative halls and figured out effective ways to organize that they got the vote and kept it, in turn setting in motion the nationwide victory for women's suffrage. As a subplot, we see Eloise and Adele joining these efforts throughout the series.

More importantly, to the plot are the murders that happen in books two and three. While there are plenty of reasons for violence in this Wild West town, historical events lay the background for motives.

Violence against the natives was more than racism. Indians inhabited, rich old-growth forests that the lumber mills were exploring, and many people called for revenge for killings by members of the Nez Perce tribes. **So in 1871** – the S'Klallam village of Qatay was burned by order of the federal government.

Other motives included drugs, opium to be exact. Smuggling created a cat-and-mouse conflict between smugglers and the customs agents who chased them. These pursuits were the stuff of local news and legend alike. One way to smuggle goods was to anchor north of what is now North Beach and west of modern Fort Worden. Goods and people were lowered into small boats and rowed stealthily to shore for transport inland. The ship then continued to port with the remaining, legitimate cargo. We'll see a couple of our characters en route to a cave along shore.

Stories are told of the best sailors, who knew the waters like the back of their hands and could steer through the blackest nights. The customs agents had faster, well-armed ships, yet often they could only watch for contraband after it had already reached the shore. The earliest merchant vessels had brought supplies from across the Pacific or down from British Columbia to the Washington Territory without restriction.

As the region became prosperous, it also became subject to taxes, which the earliest settlers resented. The customs house at Port Townsend was set up and ready to collect taxes by keeping a close watch on smugglers. Money has always been a motive for murder.

And then came crimping

Port Townsend's "crimps" were, if anything, more like dishonest businessmen, even though such occurrences might have happened. We'll see them in play in this series. Having been paid and released, the sailors came ashore, their pockets full of money. In the port town, a crimp was always nearby, eager to offer a weary traveler lodging and food. The rates seemed reasonable with full pockets, but the clinking of coins eventually ceased. The crimp extended credit, and the smell of ink and paper mingled with the growing debt. Thus, the sailors are offered work on the ships of the crimp's other clientele in return for paying the debt. Not as bad as being shanghaied, which also occurred, but equally devastating to a poor sailor trying to be freed of debt.

We've mentioned the Chinese Exclusion Act

"It is a mystery precisely when the first Chinese arrived to Port Townsend, but according to the town's newspaper, there was a Chinese wash house in the 1860s … In the 1880s, there was an estimated 500 Chinese in Port Townsend. Gradually, as more Chinese arrived, a Chinese section emerged in lower Port Townsend near the waterfront, along Washington and Water Streets." — Art and Doug Chin, in their book Chinese in Washington State.

Like many other cultural communities in early Port Townsend,

Chinese, and Chinese American merchants, families, farmers, and laborers were an important part of the cultural and economic landscape of this boom town. One of many Chinese-owned businesses, the Zee Tai Company was on the books as the most prosperous business in the city in the 1890s.

The Chinese Exclusion Act of 1882 was a discriminatory federal law that prohibited the immigration of Chinese laborers until finally being repealed by the Magnuson Act of 1943. except Chinese people born in the United States, as well as merchants and their families, all Chinese laborers were banned from entering the United States. People needed to carry written proof that they were in the country prior to 1882, and without this documentation, Chinese people faced mass deportation upon arrival at Port Townsend.

As I write this series, more historical trivia will be included in future books.

Thanks for reading!

Acknowledgments

Without the support of other authors, family and friends, writing novel, for me, is harder than it should be. Sometimes I like to throw my ideas out there, or read a passage of what I'm working on, or discuss plotholes, or brain storm some "what ifs". I have been blessed with people who don't hang up on me or block my Facebook chats because I get too noisy. Instead they see me through, ask me questions, let me know if something doesn't work. I want to thank you for that! Gwen Whiting, Kim Mutch Emerson, and Lorri Moulton. You have been indispensible in helping me plog along with my insanities.

As always I thank my husband Stephen Gardner who comes peeking in at me in the middle of the night to see if I'm coming to bed yet, or makes me orange juice while I'm in the midst of a literary crisis.

Bio

Dianne Gardner is an accomplished artist, novelist, and screenwriter who dabbles in film making. She's been an artist since she was a child, and has been an apprentice to world-renown artists. Her forte is portraiture and figure, but she also loves to plein air paint.

Dianne has had a passion for the written word, having indulged in poetry in her young years and loving to write essays at school. She began writing novels in 2013. Dianne writes primarily fantasy novels including all sub-genres, with a love for historical fantasy, but has also written a historical novel based on actual letters by a relative during World War II.

All my work can be found on my website
https://gardnersart.com

More Novels by D.L. Gardner

Sword of Cho Nisi

Book 1 Rise of the Tobian Princess
Book 2 Fall of a King
Book 3 Curse of Mt. Ream
Book 4 Darkness Holds the Son
Book 5 The Keeper
Book 6 Another Man's Storm
Hoarfrost to Roses
Night Ice
Wind in the Wilds
Ian's Realm Saga bookss 1-3
Layla 4
Diary of a Conjurer 5
Cassandra's Castle 6
Streams to Ashes 7
Lost on Taikus
Tale of the Four Wizards
Dylan
Where the Yellow Violets Grow
Thread of a Spider
An Unconventional Mr. Peadlebody
Pouraka
The Far Side of Heaven
Tales of Wonder